DEVIL IN THE HOLE

*To Vivian—
My longest running
student and one of the
best! Thanks
Best
Charli Salzberg*

DEVIL IN THE HOLE

CHARLES SALZBERG

FIVE STAR
A part of Gale, Cengage Learning

GALE
CENGAGE Learning®

Detroit • New York • San Francisco • New Haven, Conn • Waterville, Maine • London

GALE
CENGAGE Learning®

LIBRARY OF CONGRESS CATALOGING-IN-PUBLICATION DATA

Salzberg, Charles.
    Devil in the hole / Charles Salzberg. — First Edition.
        pages cm
    ISBN 978-1-4328-2696-3 (hardcover) — ISBN 1-4328-2696-4 (hardcover)
    1. Families—Death—Fiction. 2. Murder—Investigation—Fiction. I. Title.
PS3619.A443D48 2013
813'.6'dc23   2013008287

First Edition. First Printing: July 2013
Find us on Facebook– https://www.facebook.com/FiveStarCengage
Visit our website– http://www.gale.cengage.com/fivestar/
Contact Five Star™ Publishing at FiveStar@cengage.com

Printed in Mexico
1 2 3 4 5 6 7 17 16 15 14 13

DEVIL IN THE HOLE

★ ★ ★ ★ ★

PART 1
THE MURDERS

★ ★ ★ ★ ★

"Le soleil ni la mort ne peuvent se regarder fixement."
                                        —La Rochefoucauld

CHAPTER ONE:
JAMES KIRKLAND

I knew something was out of whack, only I couldn't quite put my finger on it. Just something, you know. And it wasn't only that I hadn't seen any of them for some time. I mean, they'd been living there for what, three, three and a half years, and I don't think I ever had more than a two- or three-minute conversation with any of them. And God knows, it wasn't as if I didn't try. All things considered, they were pretty good neighbors. Mostly, I guess, because they kept to themselves. Which is certainly better than having neighbors who are always minding your business, or who don't mow their lawn, or who drop in uninvited, or who throw wild parties and play loud music all night long. They weren't like that. Just the opposite, in fact. Why, with that great big front lawn and two teenage boys you'd think they'd be out there tossing a football or a Frisbee around, or something. But no. It was so quiet sometimes it was as if no one lived there at all. Though I did hear rumors that the boys had a reputation of being hell-raisers. Maybe that's why they kept such a tight lid on them when they were home. Because I can honestly say there wasn't any hell-raising going on in that house that I could see. As a matter of fact, the only way you'd know the house was occupied was when you'd see the kids going to school, or him going off to work, or her and the mother going out to shop. Or at night, when the lights were on.

Which brings me back to the house itself. And those lights. It was the middle of November, a week or so before Thanksgiving, when I first noticed it. I was coming home from work and when I glanced over there I noticed the place was lit up like a Christmas tree. It's a Georgian-style mansion, one of the nicest in the neighborhood, by the way, with something like twenty rooms, and I think the lights were on in every single one of them. But the downstairs shades were drawn tight, so all you could see was the faint outline of light around the edges of the windows, which gave it this really eerie look. Maybe they've got people over, was my first thought. But that would have been so out of character because in all the time they'd lived there I'd never seen anyone go in or out other than them. And anyway, it was absolutely quiet and there were no cars in the driveway or parked out on the street.

Just before I turned in, I looked out the window and noticed the house was still lit up, which was odd, since it was nearly midnight and, as a rule, they seemed to turn in kind of early over there.

The next night when I came home from work and I looked across the street the lights were still on. And that night, before I went to bed, after midnight, I looked out and the lights were still blazing.

After that, I made a kind of game of it. Under the pretense of getting some fresh air, I walked close to the house, as close as I could get without looking conspicuous, and listened to see if there were any sounds coming from inside. A couple of times, when I thought I heard something, I stopped to listen more carefully. But I never picked up anything that might indicate that someone was inside. And each night, when I came home from work, I made it a point to check out the house and make a note of how many lights were still burning and in which windows. I even began to search for silhouettes, shadows, anything I might interpret as a sign of life. And it wasn't long before I whipped out the old binoculars to take a look, thinking maybe I could see something, anything, that would give me a hint as to what was going on. But when my wife accused me of being a peeping Tom, I put them away, at least while she was around.

There weren't always the same number of rooms lit, but I noticed there were always fewer, never more. It was as if someone was going around that house each day turning off one light in one room, but in no discernible pattern. I began to think of that damn house during the day, while I was at work, or on the train coming home. It became a real thing with me. I even kept a notebook with a sketch of the house and notations next to each window that had a light on.

At night, I played a game. I began to think of that house as my own personal shooting gallery and, sitting on the window sill in my pajamas, while my wife was either in the bathroom or asleep, I'd choose one of the rooms and aim my imaginary rifle and *pop! pop!*, I'd shoot out one of the light bulbs. And, if the next night that particular room was dark, I'd get a tremendous rush of self-satisfaction that carried me through the whole next day. It was kind of like one of those video games my kids play. Pretty sick, huh?

I mentioned it to my wife—not my silly game, but the fact that those lights were going out one by one. She thought I was nuts. "Can't you find anything better to do with your time?" she asked.

"No," I said. "I'm entertaining myself. Leave me alone." Then I asked whether she'd seen the Hartmans lately, because I was beginning to have this weird feeling in the pit of my stomach, as if something was seriously wrong. That it wasn't a game anymore.

"No," she said. "I haven't. But that's not unusual. Besides, it's not as if I'm looking for them. If you ask me, they're creepy.

The whole bunch of them."

"I know. But maybe . . . maybe there's something wrong."

"Go to bed," she said. So I did, lulling myself to sleep with my imaginary rifle cradled in my arms, as if it would actually afford me some protection just in case something was wrong.

A few nights later, I set the alarm for three-thirty and slipped the clock under my pillow. When the vibration woke me, I got up quietly, so as not to wake my wife, looked out the window and sure enough the same number of lights was burning in the house as the night before. I was puzzled and frustrated because I was dying to know what was going on. I even thought of making up some kind of lame excuse to ring the Hartmans' bell. But I didn't have the nerve.

Two weeks later, only three rooms in the house were still lit. Down from eight the week before, fourteen the week before that, the week I began to keep count. I asked my son, David, whether he'd seen the Hartman kid in school, the one in his class.

"We're not exactly best buds, Dad," he said. "He keeps to himself. He's weird. Maybe he's queer or something."

"I just asked if you'd seen any of them lately."

"Not that I can remember. But I don't go out of my way looking for any of them. They're a bunch of weirdoes."

I went back up to my room and stared out the window for maybe fifteen minutes, trying to figure out what the hell was going on. I wondered if I should do something.

"Come to bed," my wife said.

"I'm worried," I said without taking my eyes off the Hartman house. "There's definitely something wrong over there."

"You're being ridiculous," she said. "Besides, it's none of our business."

"No, I can feel it. Something's . . ."

She sighed, got out of bed and handed me the phone. "Well,

rather than having to spend the rest of my life with a man who insists on staring out the window at the neighbors' house all night like an idiot, I'd just as soon you called the police and let them put your mind at ease. At least maybe they can get them to turn out all the lights. Maybe then we can get some sleep over here."

So, that's how I called the cops.

Chapter Two:
Officer Rick Stiles

Sedgewick is not what you'd call your high-crime area. Most of what we get here are burglaries and simple misdemeanors, like disturbing the peace and DUI. Kids, mostly, whooping it up after school. Too much free time. Too much money. Too little parental supervision. Sure, we got drug abuse, just like everywhere else, but due to the social stature of the majority of families in this area, it's kept under wraps. Which, believe me, is a pleasure, since I'm more accustomed to junkies nodding off in public parks, tenement shooting galleries, and kids no older than mine selling grass and who knows what right out in the open.

As far as burglaries are concerned, well, most houses in this area are equipped with very sophisticated alarm systems. But where there is a B & E you can be sure it's not your nickel-and-dime variety. We're talking mucho dinero up here. Jewelry, for instance, the kind you see fancy women wearing on their way to an exclusive jet-set party; and art, the kind they usually hang in museums. Not too long ago, we had this gang up here that specialized in targeting rich people's homes and stealing their jewelry. They must have been acrobats, because they sure didn't come in the front door. A few times, they even robbed the houses late at night, when folks were actually in their beds, asleep. That's how good they were. No one was the wiser till the next day, when they went looking for their valuables. No clues. Not a print. Not a hair. Not a thread. Once they even hit the same house twice in the same month. Never did catch 'em. But when there was a rash of similar thefts over in Jersey, we just figured they moved their act a little south, a little west. Smart. Very smart.

As for disturbing the peace and public intoxication, well I gotta tell you, folks up here have a very interesting way of handling it. If you're picked up for drunk driving or public intox, your name is published right there in the local rag for all your friends and family to see. "John Q. Public was stopped on Grove Lane late last night for speeding and reckless driving while under the influence of alcohol. It is the third time this month Mr. Public has been detained." Like that. I believe it has to do with peer pressure, doing the job the judicial system can't. The way it's supposed to work is that all the people you normally associate with at the country club will see your name in the paper for DUI and say, "Shame, shame," and shun you. No more invites to the Saturday night dance at the country club. No more fancy dinner parties. It's all kind of quaint, though I doubt it does much good, especially since too many people get their jollies seeing their names in print, no matter what the reason. Why do you think those losers go on shows like *American Idol*? It's all about exposure. All about being on TV. What is it now, fifteen seconds? But I guess you gotta give the idea points for creativity, using embarrassment instead of incarceration as a weapon against crime. Of course, it could never work back home, where if you stopped someone for that sort of infraction and threatened to print their name in the paper they'd just laugh in your face and then ask you to take their photograph to go along with it.

I'm cynical, I know, but that's because I'm not from around here. Moved up from Queens with my family almost four years ago. I was with the NYPD eleven years. Finally got so bad I couldn't take it no more. 9/11 was kind of the last straw. So, after a year of looking for the right situation, I chucked the old pension and we packed our bags and moved up here to Sedgewick. It was like moving to another planet. Not that I actually live here—much too ritzy for our meager bank account. We have a small house inland, a two-family job that brings in some extra income from the rental. Not far from New Haven, in a working-class community, maybe forty-five minutes from the shore.

Connecticut was a big change for us. The difference was like night and day. One day we're wading knee-deep in a wasteland of granite and garbage, the next we're surrounded by trees, grass, flowers, roadside vendors selling fresh vegetables I'd never seen outside cellophane wrapping or cardboard boxes. As a bonus, we've got the gentle, slightly polluted waters of the Long Island Sound.

Before moving up here I had a preconceived notion of what things would be like. I always associated Cee Tee with cute blondes in pastel-colored cotton sweaters with dainty little powder-blue flowers around the neckline driving around in red BMWs, or sailing on expensive yachts. And when I got here, I found that wasn't so far from the truth.

Occasionally, though, in the middle of all the sunshine and flowers, we get a rape, a wife-beating, or even a homicide. But mostly it's cruising around, handing out moving-violation citations, making sure everything is a-okay in Wonderland, generally giving folks a false sense of security, as if the real world out there can never intrude. Real crime happens in the City, or on TV. Not up here, unless you count a politician on the take, but then that ain't particularly newsworthy anymore, is it?

It's the kind of job that could actually put an extra five, ten years on my career, and the pay ain't all that bad either, even though my wife does have to work part time in New Haven as a legal secretary just so's we can stay a little ahead of the game.

That night kind of changed everything, though. It was about eleven o'clock P.M. and my partner, Phil Schuster, and I were parked in front of the D.Q. just outside town. We were bullshitting about this and that, keeping an eye on the kids hanging out, just to nip any trouble in the bud, if you know what I mean, when a call came in ordering us to number 541 Oakdale Drive, home of a Mr. James Kirkland. When we got there, Phil, he was driving, stayed in the car while I went up to the house. I was met by Mr. Kirkland, dressed in pajamas and a bathrobe. He said there seemed to be no signs of life in the house across the street and that it had been that way for some time.

"I know this must sound silly, Officer,"—I love it when they call me officer, not like down in the City, where I wouldn't want to repeat the kinds of things they call us—"but it's been bugging the hell out of me for weeks now."

"No problem, sir," I said. "We'll just go over, knock on the door, and make sure everything's all right."

"Thank you," he said, and he looked relieved. I pegged him as just another nosy neighbor, but what the hell.

I went back to the car, pulled Schuster out, told him the problem, and we both walked up to number 438 Oakdale Drive together. We had a laugh because usually we get complaints about too much noise, not complaints that there isn't any.

I knocked on the door, but received no answer. I knocked again, this time harder. I called out the name of the owner of the house, John Hartman, a couple times. Still no response. Phil suggested we walk around back to see if we could rouse a response there. We did, but like before, no one answered. We went back around to the front trying to look in windows along the way, but the draperies and shades were drawn tight and all the lights downstairs were out. As a matter of fact, the only light left on in the house was in what we assumed was an upstairs bedroom. Phil stood back on the lawn and started throwing small pebbles up at the window, trying to get someone's attention. Plink. Plink. Plink. He was right on target, but still there was no response.

We went back to the front door and Phil put his head up close, listening for some sound from inside. "Damn," he said, backing away quickly. "It smells like hell in there."

"Let's see," I said, putting my head closer to the door. "What the hell you think that is?" I asked, rubbing my nose to get rid of the stench.

"I don't think I want to know," Phil mumbled, but from the way he looked I could see he had a pretty fair idea of what it was. And then so did I.

"Maybe we oughtta break in," I said.

"Yeah, I guess," said Phil, who seemed a little spacey all of a sudden. So we did. I used my nightstick to crack one of the window panes. Then Phil, who's smaller than me, crawled in through the window and let me in the front door.

Inside, it was cold, pitch dark and the smell was real strong. Kind of sour, like rotting food or a dead animal carcass. I looked for a light switch, but when I found it and flicked it back and forth, nothing happened. We didn't want to disturb anything, so we took out our flashlights and began to search the house, which was surprisingly bare of furniture, as if someone was either moving in or out.

It didn't take long before we got into what we later found was called the ballroom. It was there that we saw it. I gagged. Phil, cool as a cucumber, said, "Go out and call in." So I did. I don't remember how I got from the house back to the car, which was a good thirty, forty yards, but I was panting when I got there so I must've run.

When I raised the dispatcher, I said: "You'd better send help out here. There's been a mass murder."

CHAPTER THREE:
OFFICER PHIL SCHUSTER

As soon as I caught a whiff, it all came back to me. Like it was yesterday. I was only a kid, nineteen, but a smell like that stays with you forever. It's like when you go to the dentist for the first time and you get a shot of Novocain. No matter where you are or what you're doing, you get a whiff of that smell again and you're back in the dentist's chair, just like that first time.

That's how it was that night at the Hartman house. The smell of death took me back to 'Nam. It's like I was riding a time machine. Mostly it's a blur now—hell, it's been more than thirty years—and I don't really like to talk about it, but I remember that smell, that putrid, stomach-turning smell of rotting flesh that permeated the air—only add to that the after-burn stench. It got so bad it permeated the fibers of what you were wearing. It was always there, clinging to your clothing, your rifle and even worse, inside your head.

Sometimes, even now, I get nightmares. I dream of being buried alive under a mountain of human carcasses and when I wake up that horrible stink of death is in my nose, just like when I was over there. And this is really weird—I can even smell it on my sheets and pajamas when I wake up in the morning. That's how strong it is . . . and how real. I just can't seem to get rid of it. Weird, huh?

Anyway, that's what was coming from inside that house. That smell.

Once we got inside it didn't take long to trace it to a large room off the main hallway. There, on the parquet floor, each one of them was lying on his own individual blanket. Four of them. A woman and three kids. Teenagers, it looked like. Two boys and a girl. The weird thing was, they looked so peaceful lying there on their backs, arms by their sides, eyes closed, like they were asleep. But they weren't asleep. They were dead. No doubt about that.

There wasn't much blood. Each victim appeared to have just one bullet hole in the head, just slightly above the right temple. It was remarkably symmetrical, and that made it even more horrifying. And creepy.

I could see Stiles was pretty shook up. And it's funny, him being the tough kid from the big city, the guy who's supposed to have seen everything at least twice. At least that's what he's always telling me. And here he was having trouble holding himself together. I thought for sure he was going to toss his cookies, so I sent him out to the car to call in. I figured he needed the fresh air.

Meanwhile, I stood around a couple seconds, just staring at their faces, which were already showing signs of decay. You know what I was thinking about? My own death. That's what. When I was nineteen, like all kids, I thought I was immortal. But one lousy day in Viet Nam changed all that. I became obsessed with death. I thought about it all the time. And when I finally got back home, I couldn't even drive a car because I kept having visions of automobile accidents with twisted bodies being consumed by flames. I'd get in that damn car and my hands would shake, I'd break out in a cold sweat, and I'd get these terrible migraines. I couldn't even drive over a bridge or through a tunnel with someone else at the wheel without imagining all sorts of catastrophic disasters. What if the bridge collapsed? What if the tunnel caved in? What if I was crossing the street and a car went out of control and hit me? What if . . . ? My life was filled with what-ifs. I couldn't go out of my house without imagining what kind of death I'd meet that day. It got so bad I'd think of excuses not to leave the house. I was a prisoner of my own fears.

It took years before I could shake those feelings. Maybe that's why I wound up a cop. So I could constantly challenge death, just so's I could keep it away.

Every once in a while, the feeling returns, and when I looked at those bodies lying at my feet, lined up so neat, I had to admit I didn't think of their deaths, but of mine. I'm only fifty-two, but my dad croaked when he was fifty-two. Bad ticker. You know what they say about genetics. Maybe I'm living on borrowed time. Yeah, I can practically hear my clock ticking.

So I made myself turn away. I took a look around the rest of the house. I went through the first floor and then remembered there'd been a light burning upstairs, so I went up there. The door was closed. The smell was there, too, so I didn't bother to unholster my gun. I opened the door slowly and there, lying on the bed with the covers tucked neatly up around her neck, was another one, an old woman, in her late seventies, her bluish-gray hair perfectly coifed, her hands folded peacefully across her chest, a diamond ring and gold wedding band still on her finger. She also looked as if she were sleeping. I closed the door gently and, like a fool, quietly tiptoed through the rest of the house. I'd just found another victim, what was left of an Irish setter (it seemed to have decomposed at a faster rate than the other bodies), when I heard Rick calling me from downstairs.

I made my way back to the top of the stairs and whispered, though God knows why since there was no one alive to disturb, "It's all right. I'll be right down."

When I got downstairs Rick was standing by the door. His face was pale and he was chewing on his fingernails. "Did you call it in?" I asked.

"Uh-huh," he said, looking past me toward the ballroom, as if someone was going to step out of there any moment. "Anything up there?"

"Another one," I said. "And a dog."

He started to gag, but caught himself. "My God," he said, "who could do something like this?"

"Some kind of maniac, I guess," I said, noticing for the first time that Rick had left the front door ajar, probably to air out the house. I didn't have the heart to tell him it was futile. I didn't have the heart to tell him that smell would be in the house forever, embedded in the woodwork, the walls, even the floors.

Yup, the smell of death is almost impossible to get rid of. You can try, but it's still gonna be there. Forever.

CHAPTER FOUR:
JAMES KIRKLAND

To be honest, I have to admit, it was all very exciting.

I watched them ring the doorbell and when they got no response they went around back. A minute later, they were back in front again, and when I saw them break into the house I could hardly contain myself. I turned to my wife and said, "I knew it. I knew there was something wrong. I'm going over there."

"Oh, no you're not," she said, grabbing my arm. "It's police business now, so butt out."

"I've seen it this far, so I guess I'll see it all the way," I said, taking back my arm. "Besides, aren't you curious?"

"I'm sure we'll all find out soon enough."

"I'm going." I grabbed my windbreaker from the hall closet and practically sprinted toward the door.

I left the house just in time to see one of the officers run from the neighbors' house to his car. Like he was shot from a cannon, that's how fast he was moving. He opened the front door on the passenger's side, the side closest to the house, reached in, grabbed the mike, and began talking. I tried to make out what he was saying, but all I could hear was static. I hung back in our doorway a moment or two until he finished, and then watched him go back inside before I crossed the street.

When I got to the Hartman house, the door was partially open and there was a godawful odor coming from inside. I didn't want to just barge in like some neighborhood busybody, so I put both hands on the door frame, leaned in and called out, "Everything all right in there?"

I got no answer. I let a moment pass, then I repeated, "Hey, everything all right in there?" Then I took a step or two inside the house. It was pretty dark and cold, colder even than it was outside. I could see my breath and I remember wishing I'd taken an overcoat instead of that flimsy windbreaker. It was very quiet and I had this eerie feeling. I was about to go a little further inside when one of the officers suddenly appeared with a flashlight and shined it in my face.

He looked at me as if he were trying to recognize who I was, and then he said with a slight catch in his voice, "I'm sorry, Mr. Kirkland, but you'll have to leave."

"What happened?" I asked, though I knew someone was dead inside that house.

"Please, Mr. Kirkland, we have to keep this area clear. This is a crime scene and there's a police investigation under way. We can't have people tramping over possible evidence."

"I just wanted to see what was going on," I said. Just then I heard the wail of police sirens coming up the street. I looked over my shoulder as three squad cars screeched to a halt in front of the house. Half a dozen cops jumped out and ran up the walk, their hands on their holsters, just like on TV.

"Please, go back to your house," the cop said, almost begging. I stepped aside to let the other police officers pass.

All hell was breaking loose now. Two more police cars, sirens blasting, arrived along with two ambulances. By this time the neighborhood was so lit up it looked like a movie set. Everyone was wide awake and either outside on their front lawn or standing in the street in front of the Hartman house. There was even a small crowd gathering on the sidewalk that ran along the edge of the Hartmans' front lawn. I was the only civilian actually standing on the Hartman property and when I looked across the street in the direction of my house I saw my wife, her fur coat wrapped tightly around her nightgown, standing on our front stoop watching. I smiled and gave her a subdued wave, like the Queen of England gives her royal subjects. I felt pretty stupid afterward, but at the time it seemed the thing to do. To reassure her. Maybe even to reassure me. She motioned furiously for me to come back, but I put my hand up in a gesture that meant, "In a minute," and then returned my attention to the Hartman house. I was in the middle of everything, all the excitement, and I wasn't about to let this moment pass without finding out everything I could about what happened.

From inside I heard someone shout, "Hey, where the hell are the lights?" Another voice answered, "They're all burned out. Goddamn flashlights ain't worth shit. Go outside and see if anyone has any spare bulbs."

I told them I did. I jogged back over to my garage and returned with a dozen of various wattages. People were trying to get closer, but I was the only one they were letting through.

Ten minutes later, with most of the house lit up again, the officer who'd originally answered my call came out of the house. He was pale and perspiring heavily, even though the temperature was at the freezing mark and a sharp wind had begun to blow in off the Sound. He took off his cap and wiped his brow with the sleeve of his leather jacket.

"How many of them are in there?" I asked, hugging myself for warmth.

"Huh?"

"How many are in there?" I repeated.

"Five," he said absently.

"Oh, sweet Jesus," I said. There was this sinking feeling in my stomach because now it was all too real. "How long have they been dead?"

He shook his head. "Weeks, maybe," he said, again in the

25

same odd, disconnected tone.

"Do you know what happened?"

He shook his head no.

I was about to offer my burglary theory when I realized there were six in the Hartman family, so I asked, "Which ones?"

"Which ones?"

"I mean, who did you find? If there are only five, then someone's missing."

He didn't answer for a moment, as if making a body count in his head. "Only five in there," he said. "Name the family."

"Well, there was Mr. and Mrs. Hartman, his mother, and three kids, two boys and a girl . . ."

"There's no man," he said, looking away from me, in the direction of the Sound.

"You're sure? The bodies must be pretty well decomposed by now."

He nodded yes. "The cold must've helped preserve them," he explained.

"Oh," I said, and suddenly, seeing a mental picture of the scene inside, a wave of nausea came over me. "Where do you think he is? Hartman, I mean. Maybe you just overlooked him."

"We didn't even know . . . I'd better tell somebody." He put his cap on and walked back into the house.

By this time, the local press had arrived, and a reporter was talking to one of the police officers. As for me, the excitement was beginning to wear off a little. I was shivering, the cold slicing through me like a knife. And my legs started to feel a little rubbery. It was time to go home, so I approached someone who seemed to be in charge, told him who I was and that I was going back to my house so that if anyone wanted to question me, that's where I'd be. He said he thought they would, but probably not until morning.

I went home. My wife tried to get me upstairs, but I was

much too keyed up. I sat by the fire a while, trying to warm up, thinking about the Hartmans, about something that horrendous happening right next door, about those bodies lying there for God knows how long. I kept going over the past three weeks in my mind, trying to remember everything, every little detail, especially everything about the first night I'd noticed the lights on, so I could be of some help to the cops; and also so I could tell it all to anyone who asked. I wanted to get it right. After all, things like this don't happen every day.

Finally, I realized I had to get up the next morning for work, so I went upstairs. By this time my wife was fast asleep. I didn't fall off until almost three-thirty in the morning, and that was one full hour after the police finally left the crime scene. Just before I did fall asleep, I got out of bed and went to the window. I looked over at the Hartman house. I wanted to make sure it wasn't all a dream.

As if to prove it wasn't, there was still one lone police car sitting quietly out front, its headlights extinguished so that now, for the first time in almost three weeks, the house across the street was completely dark.

Not a single light burning.

Chapter Five:
Chief of Police Sanders

I like to think of myself as a philosophical fellow, you know, the kind who sits around the banks of the Connecticut River with a fishing pole contemplating the loftier issues of life, until I get a bite on my line. Only then is it time to reel in the catch. I throw 'em back in. To be honest, I don't even like fish all that much.

I believe most things that happen have a good side and a bad. It just depends which side of the river you're on. For instance, for some folks this Hartman thing would have been the chance of a lifetime, an opportunity to climb up a rung or two on the ladder of success. But for me, it was just a royal pain in the ass.

It wasn't just the murders—murder's always a nasty business—it was what went along with it. A nice, neat little homicide, well, that's one thing. But this was something else. First off, something like this is impossible to keep quiet. It had all the earmarks of a sensational case—well-to-do family, wealthy suburban community, violent unexplained deaths, father slash husband missing—and that meant publicity and lots of it. Newspaper reporters, television crews, photographers, press conferences. The works. And sure enough, within a day we made all the New York City papers. It was even the lead story on both the six and eleven o'clock news. We even made the third story on the NBC Nightly News, and Katie Couric even mentioned us just before the first commercial break. There was no turning back now.

For someone more ambitious than me, this would have been great. But at that point in my life I wanted one thing and one thing only: Do my job and then, when the time came, collect my pension and move down south where the climate is a bit more hospitable.

This sort of thing not only gives the whole community a black eye, but it also produces enormous pressure. Pressure to solve the case; pressure to apprehend the perpetrator; pressure to convict; pressure to sentence. Pressure, period. It would have been so much simpler if the sonuvabitch had just pulled his own plug after he finished with his family. But no such luck.

I got the call just as my wife and I were settling in to watch Leno.

"Shit," I said after I hung up, sorry that I hadn't let the machine take the message. But I went right out there anyway, knowing it would look bad if I didn't.

It was, for all the care, neatness and obvious planning that went into it, still a gruesome sight. Maybe it was the sheer meticulousness of it all that made it so gruesome. Somehow, the bloodier the murder is, the more understandable it is. Murder without blood and disarray hardly seems like murder at all. It's more like . . . a play, if you know what I mean.

It's these damned malice aforethought things that really get to you. I believe we're all capable of crimes of passion, given the right circumstances, but it takes a special kind of human being to commit something as cold-blooded as this. And to murder your own? Well, that's just incomprehensible.

We did the preliminary work in an hour or so, then came back the next morning to finish up. We were three, maybe four hours dusting for prints, looking for clues, signs of forced entry, what have you, even another corpse, because none of us, even the most cynical, could believe anyone in his right mind could do that sort of thing to his own flesh and blood. Maybe, we kept telling ourselves as we searched the basement and backyard for signs of recent digging, we'd find John Hartman's body somewhere.

But we didn't. Everything pointed directly to him as the killer. First of all, and probably most damaging, he wasn't there and these murders, you'll recall, had taken place a good three weeks earlier. Second, we found a pistol, newly cleaned and oiled, in the top drawer of a small table in the hallway, and another one upstairs in the master bedroom. We didn't know if either was the actual murder weapon, but it wouldn't take long to find out.

One curious thing we did find, though, were bullet holes scattered throughout various parts of the house, both upstairs and down, in the woodwork and walls. It was almost as if the house itself was under attack. Like some kind of holy war had taken place. Only we could find absolutely no signs of a struggle, which led us to believe that Hartman or whoever committed the murders must have either drugged the victims, then murdered them in their sleep with some sort of silencing device; or they submitted willingly, which was highly unlikely. By the way, we never released that fact to the press, because we wanted to have something that only the killer would know.

We had all kinds of questions, not the least of which was why it had taken three weeks for the murders to be discovered. Why weren't the kids missed at school? And surely Mrs. Hartman had friends who wondered where she was all that time? Why wasn't there any mail in the mailbox? Newspapers piled at the door? Why no car in the driveway? Where was it? Had Hartman used it to make his getaway? Why were there no shell casings in the house? There must have been close to two dozen shots fired, yet we only had the slugs.

But first things first. Since we had a suspect, our first job was to compile a comprehensive profile of him in an effort to locate his whereabouts. We put out an APB on him across the country, and then began a long series of interviews with friends, neighbors and anyone who might have had even the slightest contact with him.

That evening though, before I could give myself an ulcer, I got good news. The State of Connecticut along with the FBI was going to take over the case.

It was the best Christmas present I could have received.

CHAPTER SIX:
CHARLIE FLOYD

Call me crass, like I'm some kind of ghoul or something, but there's nothing I like better than sinking my teeth into a nice, juicy murder. It gets the blood boiling, the adrenaline pumping. So naturally, when I heard about the Hartman murders on the car radio as I was driving to work, I put a little extra pedal to the metal and made it there in record time.

Since I'm one of the senior investigators on staff, I can pretty much pick and choose the cases I want. And this was one I wanted. Bad. I'm not ashamed of it. I like the limelight. I like to be quoted. I like to stand out in a crowd. That's why I dress the way I do. I get shit for it, sure. People don't always like me. You think I give a shit? No. Because they do have an opinion about me and that's what I care about. It's not that I'm full of myself, or some kind of publicity-seeking asshole; it's just that I do better work when I think of myself as a star. It gives me something to live up to. You think A-Rod doesn't think he's the best? Or Pujols? Sure they do. And that's part of what makes them the best.

It was obvious who the murderer was. We just had to find him and bring him in. And part of that was figuring out why he did it, because that would probably help us accomplish the first part. Normally, these are not the kinds of cases I have the hots for. I like puzzles. I like putting pieces together. I really get off on it. This? Well, this was just a matter of chasing him down. Then hauling his ass back up here to face the music.

Most crimes are fairly cut and dried. Like a homicide committed during the commission of a Class A felony, or a family killing, usually accomplished, by the way, with a handy kitchen utensil. It's simply a matter of coming up with enough physical or forensic evidence so the prosecution doesn't fall flat on its face during the trial, or just plain screw up, which has happened to me more than once.

It's hard work, believe me, and I'm not just saying that to blow my own horn or blow smoke up your ass. And it's not the least bit glamorous, which is why, once in a while, I like those star-quality cases. It's the painstaking process of interviewing witnesses and following up leads, most of which turn out to mean shit. Tedium, pure tedium. But I love it. Because when things click, when you come up with that piece of evidence that absolutely nails the son-of-a-bitch to the wall, you feel terrific. It's like having a fucking great orgasm. And how often does that happen?

I think it was Mark Twain who once said, "If the desire to kill and the opportunity came always together, who would escape hanging?" And it's true. Fortunately, not too many of us play out this kind of fantasy. Video games have done that job for us. The arcades are filled with kids on killing sprees. But when someone actually does it for real, I wanna be the one to catch them.

So I caught the Hartman case, but I wasn't alone. I had the "help," you can put that in quotes, of the local and state authorities of which, technically, I am one. But in addition, there was the FBI, even Interpol, because two days after the bodies were discovered we got a call from the NYPD telling us that the suspect's dark blue Honda Accord had been found abandoned in a parking lot at Kennedy Airport.

Under some circumstances, I suppose this might be taken as a false clue to steer us in the wrong direction, but since we figured our boy had every reason to believe the bodies of his victims wouldn't be found for some time, it was logical that he actually did hop a plane for somewheres. And he had plenty of time to make his escape, since the coroner placed the time of deaths on or about November 6, almost a month earlier.

What fascinated me was the state of mind of the killer and his motive. I can understand crimes of passion, crimes that come out of ignorance or hatred, crimes committed by the mentally disturbed, which are crimes that seemingly have no rhyme or reason. And I can certainly understand crimes of monetary aggrandizement—someone's got something you want, won't give it to you, so you take it and then maybe things get out of hand. But what I can't understand is something like this, something so well planned and carried out with such precision. Enough time to sit around and clean the fucking murder weapon and lay out the bodies like he was laying out a bunch of towels to dry. He even thought of stopping the mail delivery. It's sick, maybe, but this was someone I had to meet. And for this reason, I prayed he was still alive, just so I could look him in the eyes.

After a week of intensive investigation, we had a folder full of information on Hartman and his family, none of which would go a long way in helping us find him.

First, the murder scene: four victims, three kids and a woman had been murdered in the ballroom, placed on blankets folded precisely in half, one to a blanket. Hartman's mother had been murdered in her bedroom, while she slept. Each victim died instantly, one bullet fired from point-blank range into the brain, precisely in the same spot in each victim.

We came up with two weapons, a .32 caliber revolver, found by the cops searching the house that night, and a 9 mm pistol found the next day in the upstairs master bedroom. Both had been cleaned and oiled after they'd been fired. The .32 caliber piece was used in the murders. The other had been fired into various locations throughout the house. God only knows why.

The house. That was another thing. It was sparsely furnished, making it hard to believe it'd been lived in for nearly four years. It was in an advanced state of decay and disrepair. In short, it looked like shit, even if it was immaculately clean. The ceilings were crumbling, the paint peeling, and various major and minor repairs were obviously needed. There were three separate mortgages on the house: one for $120,000; one for $90,000; and one taken out recently for another seventy-five grand. The house had cost $500,000 when Hartman purchased it, and now, according to a local real estate agent, it was worth at least four times that. As far as I could tell, it was a case of someone living far beyond his means. Did he play the horses? Drink? Do drugs? Play around on the side? We didn't know yet, but we would.

Hartman himself was forty-eight years of age, five-ten, 160 pounds, give or take a few. Photographs were hard to come by. There were a couple left around the house, but he'd carefully cut himself out of them. While we searched for photos from the family, we made do with descriptions provided by neighbors and co-workers. He wore his brown-peppered-with-gray hair short. He was clean-shaven with no identifying scars or birthmarks. He was born and raised in Illinois, a suburb just outside Chicago, and received a B.S. and M.B.A. from the University of Chicago. He majored in accounting, received his advanced degree in business administration, and was a good enough student to graduate cum laude. He was in the army, stationed in Germany. For the past ten years or so he'd worked as a computer analyst, the last four for Xerox, before that six years for a financial consulting firm in Syracuse. His salary was seventy-two thousand bucks, clearly not enough to cover his mounting expenses. His only living relative was a married sister who still lived in the Chicago area.

Adele Hartman was a nondescript woman who, we learned from relatives, including a sister living in North Carolina, had been married once before. She was generally described as a pleasant enough woman who underwent a drastic personality change approximately two years earlier when she had what one neighbor described as a "nervous breakdown." After that, the neighbor said, "She seemed more and more withdrawn, unfriendly and preoccupied." We located and interviewed the shrink who treated her, but he wasn't much help. He told us she was suffering from "anxiety attacks due to extremely low self-image." She and half the fucking female population of Connecticut, including my ex-wife.

The family kept a pretty low profile, including the kids: Edward, sixteen; Kathy, fifteen; and Paul, thirteen.

The rest of the folder, which was getting thicker by the minute, contained mostly technical stuff, all of it, I might add, pinning John Hartman to the proverbial wall.

Finding him, though, was going to be another matter.

★ ★ ★ ★ ★

PART 2
THE MURDERER

★ ★ ★ ★ ★

"Self-love, the spring of motion, acts the soul;
Reason's company balance rules the whole.
Man, but for that, no action could attend,
And, but for this were active to no end:
Fix'd like a plant on his peculiar spot,
To draw nutrition, propagate, and rot;
Or, meteor-like, flame lawless thro' the void,
Destroying others, by himself destroy'd."

—Alexander Pope

CHAPTER SEVEN:
REVEREND CHAPMAN

When I first learned of this whole mess I was, of course, utterly shocked. Frankly, I thought it had to be some kind of monstrous mistake. But no, there it was in black and white, right on the front page of the *Sedgewick Times:* "Sedgewick Man Murders Family, Disappears."

I was sitting at breakfast, lingering over a second cup of coffee, catching up on the day's events, and I said to my wife, "Did you see this?"

"What?" she asked as she finished clearing the breakfast dishes.

"This," I said, pointing to the paper. "On the front page. About the Hartmans."

"I don't have time to read the paper before three," she snapped. "And sometimes not at all. Truth is, I could use some help around here, and I don't mean Him," she said, looking up.

"We've been through all that. How would it look if we had servants?"

"Servants? Oh, please. We're talking about a housekeeper and frankly, I don't give a damn how it would look."

"It just doesn't seem right under the circumstances, but I'll give it some thought."

"I wish you would. Now what was it you were saying about the Hartmans?"

"Look at this."

Her jaw dropped. "Oh, my God," she said, "I don't believe it."

My reaction precisely. Not that I knew him all that well, of course. It's difficult for a man of the cloth to have friends, in the usual sense of the word. Probably because folks don't actually think of us as people, per se. I mean, they're terribly self-conscious around us, always on their best behavior, apologizing for this and that. They find it difficult even to have a normal conversation around us without constant self-editing. I can't say I blame them. It goes with the territory, I'm afraid.

But John Hartman was the kind of man I could have been friends with if circumstances hadn't been what they were. You might even say I admired him, from a distance, that is. He was intelligent, well read, gentle, soft-spoken, well mannered, and thoughtful in every sense of the word. A good son, a good husband, and a fine father. At least from what I could gather, though I suppose it's impossible to know exactly what goes on behind bedroom walls.

It was possible, though, that John hadn't committed the murders. I mean, all they had to go on was the fact that he wasn't in the house and they couldn't find any sign of him. Well, there was nothing that said he couldn't have been kidnapped. Or murdered, too, only elsewhere, and be buried somewhere out in the woods, or be floating in the Sound.

But when they found that car at the airport . . .

The truth is, deep in my heart of hearts, I knew even then that John had committed those murders, though I hadn't the foggiest notion what might have driven him to it. And this disturbed me because I'm the kind of person who likes to think everything turns out for the best. What could possibly make someone do something as horrible as that, I ask myself again and again? The taking of a life, under any circumstances, even self-defense, is bad enough. But to kill members of your own family in cold blood? He must have been mad. No sane person could even contemplate something as evil as that.

"You knew him," said my wife as she scraped clean the last of the breakfast dishes, "would you have thought him capable of something like that?"

I shook my head as I tried to think back to our last conversation, for some oblique hint of murder, perhaps. "No, certainly not. I have to believe this is a mistake. . . . But maybe I'm wrong."

"Not likely a mistake," said my wife as she dried her hands on her apron. "What's this world coming to?"

"I hope that's a rhetorical question."

She stared at me a moment. "You're supposed to have all the answers, aren't you?"

What could I say? I didn't want to start another argument over this. We stared at each other several moments, each waiting for the other to say something. But there was nothing to say. I had no idea what she was thinking, but I do know what I was thinking: I was wondering why life had to be so damn complicated, why there really wasn't some way to get all the answers. Finally, I said, "Do you think I ought to contact the police?"

"What for?"

"Because I'm sure they'll want to talk to me."

She shrugged. "Let them come to you." She went back to the sink and began running water over the dishes. "It gives me the shivers just thinking about it, just thinking about a man like that living right here in Sedgewick, sitting right there in church with us. I suppose you never know, do you?"

"No," I said as I rubbed the headline hard with my thumb, as if to erase it. "I suppose you don't."

I met John Hartman for the first time several weeks after he and his family moved to town. A member of my congregation happened to be the real estate agent and approached me one day and said, "Reverend, I thought you'd like to know there's a new family moving into the old Shaw house." I like to welcome new families into the area and, if they're of the same faith, invite them to visit our church and eventually, if they're of a mind, to become members of our congregation. It's part of my job, you see. Cynics, and there are plenty of them today, might think of me as, well, a salesman for God. Or worse. A huckster. A pimp. Believe me, I've been called that . . . and worse. But that's all right because, in effect, I suppose that's what I am, and I'm not ashamed to admit it. It's for a good cause and what are those but words, anyway?

It's not that I simply like having a large church, you understand, like it's some kind of divine contest to see who can chalk up the most members and earn points in heaven. It's not an ego trip or anything like that, either. It's rather that we need it. There are a great many things to be accomplished and, unfortunately, the facts of life are that they cannot be accomplished without money. This is a very wealthy community; some of the wealthiest people in the state live here, in fact, and I believe they . . . we . . . owe it to the rest of the community who may not be as well off to provide certain basic human services. This is why I like to have as large a congregation as possible and why I'm always hitting my "flock" up for contributions, something I'm always kidded about. "We gave at the office, Reverend," or "Good Lord, not again," or, "You're not playing the lottery with this money, are you, Reverend?" are some things I hear all the time. But I take it as good-natured ribbing and I persevere. Believe me, it's not a mercenary thing. It's just so we can do some good. So, that's part of why I like to meet new families, but certainly not all of it. I just enjoy meeting new people. It helps me get out of myself, I suppose.

In any case, I waited until a week or so after they moved in, so they could get settled, before I visited the Hartman house. I called first, of course, and spoke to Mrs. Hartman who, I must say, didn't seem particularly anxious to see me.

"You know, Reverend," she said in a small, fragile, tentative, remarkably bird-like voice that seemed oddly ephemeral, as though there was no body attached to it, "John's a Lutheran and I'm Catholic."

"That's quite all right," I said. "This isn't necessarily a religious visit. I'm not out to convert anybody. I just wanted to welcome you and your family to the neighborhood and perhaps answer any questions you might have. It's always helpful to get an insider's view."

"Well," she said, hesitating slightly, "I suppose it would be all right."

"Is tomorrow evening convenient? After supper, perhaps. Around eight?" I was pressing, I know, but it was for their own good. They'd thank me later, even if they never joined the congregation. There was an ominous silence and I thought perhaps she'd disappeared into the phone lines. That's how small her voice was.

Finally, she said, "Yes . . . I suppose that's all right. I'll tell John when he gets home tonight."

When I arrived the next evening it was Mr. Hartman who met me at the door. He was slim and though I wouldn't actually call him handsome, he was a pleasant enough looking man. His hair was cut short and he was dressed in a conservative dark blue suit, white button-down shirt, and a maroon and white striped rep tie, the kind of outfit that might be worn either by a prep school student or Wall Street banker. At first glance he had the appearance of a young man in his late thirties, but upon looking closer I detected deep lines in his forehead and around his eyes and mouth, which led me to believe that he was at least a decade older. He was smiling politely, but it seemed as if his mind was elsewhere.

43

"I can come back, if this is a bad time," I said. "It looks like I've caught you just as you got home from work. Perhaps you haven't even had time to eat yet."

"Oh, no," he said. "I've been home for hours. Please come in."

He led me into the large living room, but I was surprised to find that it had in it only a small, well-worn couch, an easy chair with the leather badly cracked, a television set, and a couple of folding chairs. I simply assumed their furnishings had not yet arrived from their former home and that they were making do as best they could.

"I'm sorry my wife won't be able to join us," he said. "I'm afraid she's not feeling well this evening."

For some reason, this didn't surprise me. From our short conversation on the phone I suspected there were many evenings Mrs. Hartman felt a bit under the weather. "Oh, my, I'm sorry. I hope it's not because of me. She made it quite a point to let me know she wasn't a Lutheran . . ."

He smiled. "No, please, don't think that," he said. "It's just the move and all. The kids are having to adjust—they weren't happy about moving away from their friends—so they've been acting out a little. Nothing serious. And my wife hasn't been well lately. Together, it's a killer." He actually said that, "it's a killer."

"Well, that's good," I blurted out, but I quickly realized that wasn't what I meant to say and so I tried, rather feebly, to correct myself, which made things even worse. "I mean, not that she's ill and all, but that it's not me . . ."

John laughed, sloughing off my faux pas as if it were nothing. I laughed with him and then added, "I don't think a minister ought to frighten people."

"No," he said, "all things considered I don't suppose that's their place in the scheme of things."

A moment later, he made the offer of coffee and when I accepted he left the room, returning with some cookies—cookies, he explained that were baked by his mother, who was nowhere to be seen. It was a little eerie. This big house and five other people upstairs, and yet it seemed as if Hartman and I were the only ones there. Now, under the circumstances, who knows what condition they were in, or what they were doing.

We sat around almost an hour, discussing this and that. As it happened, we had a common interest in English literature, especially the writings of Pope and Donne, though his knowledge was far more encyclopedic than mine. This unexpected turn of conversation seemed to delight him. His face brightened, his eyes became more focused, and when we spoke of Donne he got a particular twinkle in his eye and he recited, somewhat mischievously, I thought, almost as if he wanted to see my reaction:

" 'If you would do what John Donne did,

You merge the clergy with the Id.' "

We both had a good laugh and I felt like I'd passed some kind of test. Then we launched into a discussion of Freud and psychoanalysis, which Hartman didn't think much of, by the way. We didn't get far because we were interrupted by a high-pitched woman's voice from upstairs calling, "John," several times. He got up and excused himself. When he returned I asked if everything was all right. He simply nodded with a faraway, slightly pained expression on his face.

It was then that we finally got around to the subject of religion. "Well," he said, stroking his chin, "I don't suppose I'm as religious as I ought to be, and that's what you're here for, isn't it?"

"What do you mean?"

"I mean, I'm afraid in the past few years I've pretty much lost what little faith I'd had . . . and it's a case of use it or lose it, isn't it?" He laughed nervously.

Oh, Lord, I remember thinking to myself, not another one with wavering faith. This is the part of the job I could do without. Unfortunately, it's the most important part and it's the one that seems to crop up more and more lately. It seems to be some kind of epidemic and I often wish those suffering from it would simply keep it to themselves, or at least accept their loss of faith and plow on. But that never seems to be the case. Instead, inevitably, I'm the one burdened with it. I'm the one who's put in the position of having to explain God's ways, to firm the wavering, to give directions to the lost traveler. It's a responsibility I could well do without, and one I'm not sure I'm equipped to handle.

"Ah, but you must never lose faith," I said automatically, hoping that merely by forcefully making that statement, empty as it was, the problem would disappear. "That's the whole point, isn't it?"

He thought a moment. "Sometimes it's difficult," he said, his voice lowering to a whisper. "I suppose I've picked up some bad habits lately. I'm afraid I've developed a somewhat fatalistic attitude toward life."

"Why's that?" I asked. I didn't think I could do much for him, but this loss of faith does interest me. What must it take for someone who's had it to lose it? What sort of catastrophe must strike? How does one move from point A, belief, to point B, doubt? The other way seems so much more logical to me.

"Oh, I don't know. Maybe it's just a result of frustration, a feeling of powerlessness, a dissatisfaction with the way my life is going." He waved his hand around. "I know this looks like I've got it made, but appearances can be deceiving, can't they?"

"We all experience some of that," I said, and it was true, because I was beginning to have something of that same feeling that very moment. "We have to fight against those feelings, that's all."

"I know, but . . ."

There it was. *But*. The word that has no place in religion. You can't have faith if you have buts.

". . . it's difficult to control things. There seems to be no correlation between what I do and how things turn out. I just can't seem to get a handle on things. Lately, 'Things fall part; the centre cannot hold;/The blood-dimmed tie is loosed, and everywhere/The ceremony of innocence is drowned;/The best lack all conviction, while the worst/Are full of passionate intensity.' " He smiled wryly, then added, "And I'm afraid that prayer, at least for me, doesn't seem to be the answer."

"I wasn't suggesting prayer," I said, a little irritated by the direction the conversation was taking. "But what makes you think it's not the answer?"

"Oh," he said, waving his hand, "speaking pragmatically, I have my doubts about whether it works and besides, I don't believe one ought to put oneself in a position where one has to ask anybody for anything . . . even from God. Especially from God. He's got enough on his plate, don't you think? Of course, the whole thing is predicated on whether there is a God. But we all know where you stand on that one, Reverend, so I suppose there's no sense in getting into that now." He smiled enigmatically and I wondered once again whether he was merely testing me or trying to get my goat.

"No," I said, taking his lead and, I might add, grateful for it since I'm not much good at those sorts of discussions. I wasn't prepared. Frankly, I'm not quite sure at this point even why I'm a believer, other than I just know, in that part of me where such things reside, that there is a Supreme Being. But even after all these years, it's eluded me as to how to instill that sort of belief and faith in someone else, especially someone as articulate and

47

thoughtful as John Hartman. There was something about the man that was impenetrable and at times I suspected he might be toying with me, playing intellectual games at which I'm not very adept. I wanted to like him and felt I should, but there was something about him that made it impossible to get close. Like there was a wall between him and me. Maybe it was the feeling that he was constantly judging me, waiting for me to make some kind of slip. And then he'd pounce and devour me. He made me feel uncomfortable, and I didn't like that.

In any case, it was a sticky subject with me, this loss of faith business. When I first entered the ministry I thought I knew all the answers. Not only did I know there was a God, but through a series of Aquinian conceits, I could prove it. But somehow, over the years, I seem to have forgotten how to do that and now, concerned mostly with the nuts and bolts of religion, I simply believe out of habit. And I'm afraid that to be reminded of this fact upsets me, and perhaps that's why I tried to change the subject by asking, "Do you have any children, Mr. Hartman?"

"Three," he said, holding up his fingers.

"Well, they're awfully well behaved. I've been here almost an hour now and I haven't heard a thing. You have them well trained. Perhaps you'd like to try your hand with mine."

"I don't think you want that. They're supposed to be doing their homework—the schools down here seem to be a little more advanced than those up in Syracuse—but who knows what they're really up to. And," he added, almost as an afterthought, "they're being a little extra quiet tonight because my wife is trying to rest. But stick around a while and that'll change. They can be a tough bunch."

We chatted some more, but he was fidgeting and I could sense he wanted me to leave. So I excused myself, but only after inviting him and his family to services that Sunday. He promised nothing, but surprisingly, he was there, though only with his mother.

He did come to church sporadically, sometimes with one or more of his children, never with his wife, whom I never did get an opportunity to meet. His mother, however, was far more consistent. She appeared every week, a frail, gray-haired, sour-faced woman, always impeccably dressed. She sat in the very same pew at the back of the church. But, oddly enough, we never said more than two or three words to each other. She arrived on time and left as soon as the service was over. A great many people are like that, though. Ministers make them nervous. As if we can see straight into their souls. Imagine that.

John and I never spoke of religion again and I was just as glad. Perhaps he could see it made me nervous, or perhaps he'd been able to resolve his doubts. This is what I thought when one day he approached me and offered to teach Sunday school for us. I thought this was his way of telling me he'd worked out his problems and I breathed a secret sigh of relief.

But you know, a funny thing happened to me after reading about the murders. I began to experience a nearly overwhelming sense of guilt. I blamed myself for what happened. Totally irrational, I know, but I couldn't help myself. Perhaps, I thought, if I'd been more persuasive, if I'd tried just a little harder, I might have been successful in bolstering John's faith. And if I'd been successful, if I'd been able to convince him of the existence of God, wouldn't it have been impossible for him to have committed such acts? After all, if you have a strong belief in God, in good and evil, if you will, it's virtually impossible for a man in his right mind to take the life of another human being, especially in such a ghastly fashion.

At least that's what I told myself over and over and that's why, for some time after the murders, I felt I'd not only failed

John and his family, but also myself and the duty I'd sworn to God.

As a result, almost obsessively, I returned to the Scriptures and threw myself back into my work with a passion I'd never experienced before. I almost became giddy from this immersion and, after a time, it was possible to make the feelings pass. Yet even to this day I sometimes feel I'm to blame for all that happened.

The last contact I had with John was not face to face. Two days after the bodies were discovered, I was visited by Charles Floyd, an investigator attached to the State's Attorney's office. We sat in the rectory and he questioned me rather thoroughly.

"When did you get the call, Reverend?"

"I'm not quite sure, though I could probably look it up. I believe it was the first week in November."

"The exact date would be helpful," he said, so I looked it up. It was November 5. I'd made a note of what John had told me, so I'd remember why Paul wasn't in class.

"What did he say? Exactly. If you can recall."

"Well, it wasn't a particularly memorable conversation. He simply wanted me to know that his wife was taking their children to North Carolina to visit her sister and that Paul, the youngest, wouldn't be in Sunday school for a few weeks."

"Wasn't that odd?"

"No, not particularly. That sort of thing happens all the time."

"So you didn't think anything of it?"

"Why should I? I assumed there was a perfectly good family reason for the visit, but it was really none of my business. I thought it was very considerate of him, so we shouldn't worry and take the time to phone around to find out Paul's whereabouts. You know, sometimes kids play hooky . . ." For some strange reason, perhaps because of Mr. Floyd's persistent questioning and his supercilious attitude, which I frankly found rather offensive, I suddenly found myself in the position of defending John. Without thinking, I'd thrust myself into the role of his protector, which was bizarre since almost surely he was a mass murderer, a man who deserved no defender, especially not me.

"It was considerate, all right," Mr. Floyd said sarcastically, all the while jotting mysterious things down in his small black notebook. "And that's all you can tell me about your last conversation with him?" he added, staring at me, as if trying to peer deep into my mind in an attempt to jog my memory. I think he thought I was deliberately withholding information, trying to shield John.

"That's all," I said sharply. But then I began to feel guilty again and wished I could be more helpful.

"Does it mean anything?" I asked.

Floyd shook his head noncommittally. He replaced his notebook in his coat pocket. "Maybe. Maybe not. At worst, it tells us something about his state of mind. How did he seem when you spoke to him? Was he agitated? Did he seem like he was hopped up on something?"

"It was only over the phone."

"You can still tell."

"No," I said firmly, for the thought of John on drugs seemed preposterous. He was so straight. "I don't seem to recall any difference in his tone of voice."

"You're sure?"

"Yes, I'm sure," I insisted. Once again, I was agitated by Mr. Floyd's constant badgering. The sense I got from him was that he suspected everyone was hiding something, that no one told the truth. I knew it was his job and all, but still his attitude rubbed me the wrong way. He was gruff, single-minded, driven and, I thought, a bit insensitive. Oddly enough, if someone asked me about him after our meeting I might well have said he was the sort of person capable of just the kind of crime John was suspected of committing. He was that intense, that tightly wound.

"He seemed calm, as a matter of fact, though he didn't seem anxious to indulge in any small talk. But I simply assumed he was calling from work and had other things on his mind. Do you think, Mr. Floyd, that this thing was something he'd planned for some time? Or was it a spur-of-the-moment thing, a moment of madness, maybe?"

Floyd shrugged. I could tell he was finished with me. He zipped up his parka. "We don't know anything for sure, Reverend. We don't even have all the pieces of the puzzle yet. We're not even sure those people were alive when he spoke to you. But if you're asking me what I think, I think the guy had it all planned, right down to the last dotted *i*. After all, the sonuvabitch gave himself a three-week head start, didn't he?"

I must admit that certainly gave me something to think about long after Mr. Floyd left. I kept imagining John Hartman standing there in his house, his entire family dead at his feet, calmly phoning me to tell me that Paul wouldn't be around for Sunday school. It was a gruesome thought.

The whole thing left me uneasy for the rest of that day and for a good part of the next. All things considered, I didn't much care for Mr. Floyd.

CHAPTER EIGHT:
JANIE MCCLELLAN

When I found out, I guess the first thought that went through my mind was, it could have been me.

The way I figure it, he probably just snapped. And the next minute, *bam! bam! bam!* They're all dead. Just like that. And maybe, if I'd been with him at the time, if I'd still been seeing him, I mean, I'd have been the one everyone at the office was talking about in hushed tones all that day and the next and the next.

As it was, the day after the news hit, secretaries and file clerks huddled at the water fountain, trading tidbits of information and snide remarks, and giving these weird looks while every so often they pointed at John's empty office, which had suddenly turned into a goddamn holy shrine. I half expected some clown from upstairs to put a life-size plastic dummy of John in there and then everyone could go in, pay a buck and maybe touch its cock or something for luck. The Lourdes of Connecticut. What a fucking circus! Don't you just love it?

And they had these outrageous stories about him, most of them outright lies or, at the very least, gross exaggerations. I don't know how many times I wanted to bust in and say, "No, you idiots. He wasn't like that at all," or, "Oh, you're all so full of shit!" But I was a good little girl—for a change—so I just kept my mouth shut and kept my cool. Others sure as hell didn't. His poor secretary was so whacked out by the whole thing they finally had to send her home and she didn't come back for over a week, and even then they had to reassign her to another floor. I wouldn't be surprised if she's not still going through some heavy shrink work. God knows, she could use it, even before all this shit hit the fan. Little bitch was always into everyone's business.

Anyway, it was a damn good thing no one there knew about John and me, or else I never would have gotten a moment's peace. "Gee, Janie, what was he really like? Didn't your flesh crawl when he touched you?" Stupid, asinine shit like that. And then the gawking when it finally sunk in that he was, after all, a married man playing around with a secretary. As if no one else here has done something like that. As it was, it was hard enough handling things, trying to make it look as if I was just another disinterested-interested party, amazed at how some loony-tune like that could be working right down the hall. Somehow, I was able to carry it off. How was it no one saw me trembling as I typed away and suddenly got a picture in my head of John pulling the trigger, only with me at the other end? How was it no one saw my hands shake when I thought about John and me in bed together, naked, me completely vulnerable? How was it no one seemed to notice my red-rimmed eyes, which I cleverly tried to camouflage with tons of dark eye shadow? And how was it no one saw the look of absolute fear in my eyes when I thought about the possibility of his returning one dark night, knocking on my door, and blowing my brains out?

I guess I missed my true calling: I would have made a damn good actress. But then my mother always used to call me Sarah Bernhardt. She didn't mean it in a good way.

By the way, how'd you find out about me? Oh, never mind. I guess you spoke to the cops and they told you. My life's an open book now, I suppose. Next thing you know, someone from *Entertainment Tonight* will be interviewing me. Wouldn't I just love that. Or maybe they'd make a reality show out of my life.

But that would mean there was something real about it and right now, not so much. More like surreal.

After reading all about it, everything I could lay my greedy little hands on, and digesting it, because at first it seemed like it was a movie or something, my feelings were a mixture of relief, sympathy and sorrow. Not just for his family—I never even met them, really—but for John and, most of all, for me. Because as much as I hated the idea, I was part of it. John had seen to that.

To his credit, he was totally honest with me from the start. He never lied, never gave me the usual shit married men do. Like, "I'm not married," or, "I just got divorced," or, "I'm separated," or, of course, the old standby, "I'm unhappily married and my wife doesn't understand me." You think people don't say assholey things like that anymore? Think again.

One thing about John, he was always upfront about himself. He made no promises and no excuses. And I have to thank him for that.

In the beginning, he was very stiff and formal. It was almost as if he was afraid to let go, as if someone was always watching him, rating him, waiting to criticize any wrong move he might make. He seemed to be weighing things all the time. Should I do this? Should I do that? He was, all in all, a very sad man. A real tragic figure, that's how I saw him, at least. A man who found himself in the wrong place at the wrong time. He had the soul of a romantic but, unfortunately, in this world people like him always wind up getting the short end of the stick. His reach was greater than his grasp, I suppose. But hell, that's John talking, not me. In the beginning, when I was first getting to know him, he'd say things like that all the time and I'd ask, "Who said that?" because it sounded as if I ought to know, and he'd tell me. But, after a while, he became noticeably self-conscious about it. I think he thought it pointed up the differences in our education and that bothered him because he thought it bothered me, which, believe it or not, it didn't. Anyway, after a while, I couldn't possibly remember who said what, so I gave up asking, and we were both just as happy.

Why'd he do it? Well, I guess that's the million-dollar question.

The way I see it, life finally got to be too much for poor old John. Whenever things got tough, he'd say, "The world is too much with me," and then flash this goofy smile. Once, he said "The world is too much wife me," I called him on it, and he just laughed, but then he'd substitute that word all the time. He thought it was a pretty funny joke. I think he needed that. To joke around a little, I mean. Maybe that's why he was with me. I suppose his world finally closed in around him to the point where he had to do something to bust out. But to kill your whole family like that? Well, that's a little on the extreme side, don't you think?

John was no run-of-the-mill nutcase. Far from it. He was always so super-logical about everything. Like I said, he used to weigh every goddamn thing, like each little decision was a matter of life and death. I used to kid him all the time about his lack of spontaneity. He didn't like that much. He said he couldn't afford the luxury of being spontaneous. He got very quiet and thoughtful and then, after a minute or two, he'd frown, as if this debate that was always raging in his head was finally over, and then he'd kiss me and say, kind of wistfully, "You're right."

Not that he changed, but he sure tried. And it was cute, John trying to be spontaneous, I mean, because he was so terrible at it. He just didn't know how. The seeds of his so-called responsibilities were just planted too deep.

I know I sound as if I'm not surprised by what he did, but I am, at least to an extent. What I mean is, if you looked closely into his eyes you could see there was a lot going on back there.

They were the eyes of a man close to the edge, ready to snap. He held so much crap inside. But I guess I ignored all that because there was so much more to him than that. He was kind and gentle and considerate and sensitive and smart, very smart, and even though that potential was always there, I never once saw him lose his temper, either at work or with me. I know after what he did that sounds ridiculous, but it's true.

He liked me, he said, because I made him laugh. But that was before the other things I made him do for himself . . . and me. Truth is, he didn't laugh all that much, but when he did he really got into it. He'd throw his head back and laugh so hard his face would turn red and purple and you'd think he was going to have a stroke or something. It was as if there was something inside him trying to get out and laughter was the release, a way to spit out his demons. It wasn't easy for him to laugh. You see, John had this tremendous need to succeed and when he saw he wasn't making it, that he was falling short and that life was pulling him under, he'd get frustrated and then he'd try that much harder, which only made things worse. When that happened, he'd usually retreat into himself. He'd get very quiet and that glazed look would drop like a curtain. It even affected him physically, because at those moments he actually seemed to shrink in size, as though all his muscles were constricting, making him smaller and smaller and smaller. And sometimes I think he actually wished he could just shrink away into nothingness. He was so controlled, so inside himself, that I suppose I knew, if I'd given it any thought, that sooner or later the dam would burst. And, sure enough, it did. I'm sure one day he just looked at his life, decided he couldn't take it anymore, picked up that gun and went blooey, killing everyone close to him. Maybe he even aimed it at himself. I guess it was the ultimate in spontaneity. Not that they'd done anything wrong—the truth was, he loved them all, even his wife, who was such a pain—it's just that the way I see it, he wanted to take his world with him when he went. I suppose that was selfish. I don't think he blamed his family for the pressure he was under. He blamed himself.

I think John's dead. At least I hope so. For his sake. I can't see how he could be alive, with what he did and all. On the other hand, it would be just like him to make a mystery of the whole thing, to let people think he was still alive when he wasn't. I told you he had an impish sense of humor, didn't I?

We met at work. I was someone else's secretary, but occasionally I did a little typing of his son's school reports. God forbid they should do it. From what John told me, they were all pains in the asses. High maintenance, he used to say, as if that excused their behavior. He tried to pay me for it, but I wouldn't take anything. I told him it was a hell of a lot better than sitting around all day twiddling my thumbs, or listening to the latest office bullshit.

So, instead, he asked me out for a drink. I said yes because I thought he was interesting and I had nothing better going on. He definitely had potential. He had a kind of worn, beaten, almost soulful look and that was kind of appealing. And he was very smart. And the fact that he was married, I'm ashamed to say, added a bit of excitement to the formula, and excitement was something I was definitely in need of at the time.

I was also kind of impressed by his drawing. I first noticed it one day when I passed his desk and saw him doodling on a pad. His drawings were very accomplished, especially the caricatures he did of some of the people in the office.

"Hey, not bad," I said as I leaned over his shoulder. He immediately got all embarrassed and tried to cover up the pad.

"Don't worry," I whispered, bending close to his ear, "I won't tell anybody how you spend your day, if you don't tell anybody how I spend mine."

He smiled sheepishly, like a kid who's been nabbed for raiding the cookie jar, and said, "I'm afraid I have no idea how you spend yours."

"And you're not likely to find out, either. Or my nights," I added with a wink.

That's when he cleared his throat about a dozen times and finally asked me out for a drink. Right away I knew we'd eventually wind up in the sack. John was a little too reticent and proper to make a move, though I knew he wanted to. But I wasn't. Living up in Connecticut was a little like being on vacation in a foreign country. Anything goes. Somehow, the thought of consequences never entered my mind. I just wanted to have a good time, that's all. That first evening he told me he was married, which I already knew, of course, I said, "But you'd still like to go to bed with me, wouldn't you?"

"I'm married," he repeated, though this time less emphatically.

"All things are possible, John. And to tell you the truth, I'm horny as hell."

He didn't say anything then, but a week later, after he'd thought through all the consequences, I guess, we became lovers.

As a lover John was, uh, how can I say it? Inhibited. But I'll say this for him, he wanted to please and he was a real quick learner. I know this sounds ridiculous, but I was the one who introduced him to oral sex. I mean, can you imagine, a man his age never having had a blow job? He never said so, but I think the only woman he'd ever slept with before me was his wife.

One night, when we were in my apartment together, I said to him, just in jest, "John, honey, you'd better not take any of these new tricks home with you or else your wife'll know you've been cheating on her."

I thought I'd get a laugh or at least a smile, but I didn't.

Instead, he suddenly turned self-righteous. "I'm not cheating on her," he said, his facing turning to stone.

"Sure you are," I said lightly, not realizing I'd exposed a nerve.

He turned sullen and started shrinking right before my eyes. He got out of bed and began putting on his clothes.

"Where are you going?" I asked.

"Home."

"Oh, come on, John, stop being so childish. It was only a joke. I'm sorry, okay?"

"I have to go."

"John, I said I'm sorry, so for Chrissakes stop pouting like a fucking two-year-old. You're not cheating, okay? Is that what you want to hear?" He didn't say anything, just kept on dressing. He was up to his shirt and pants now. I got down on my hands and knees and crawled over to him. "Oh, please, John, don't go. Please, please, please." I began kissing his shoes, then the cuffs of his slacks. I kept kissing right up his pant legs and then, when I got close enough, I grabbed his crotch, all the while pleading with him in my most slave-girlish voice. It was all so ridiculous that I finally managed to get a smile out of him.

"Oh, John, you're the most honest man I've ever met. You'd never cheat on anyone." He laughed and then, well, I guess that did it, because he stayed. But that night told me something about him I hadn't known before. First off, he didn't like to be reminded of his indiscretions or, to put it bluntly, that he was human, like the rest of us, and second, he was somehow able to divorce himself from reality when it suited him.

Another sore spot with John was his art. He loved to draw, but it was hell getting him to show me what he'd done. And he didn't like to talk about it, either. Once, though, I was able to get him to open up as he was driving me home one night.

"I always wanted to be a painter," he said as he stared at the road ahead. "Like Edward Hopper. But my father had other ideas. 'Art,' he used to say, 'is for those who have the time to enjoy it, or have rich parents who can afford to indulge them. You, John, have neither.' "

And heaven forbid that John should do what he wanted. So, at the urging of his father, who sounded like a class-A prick, John took all kinds of business and accounting courses. Poor John. He didn't know how to rebel. He always wanted to please, no matter what the cost.

"It's not too late," I told him.

"Yes, it is. I've got too many responsibilities. I've got a family to think about."

"If they really cared about you, they'd want what was best for you," which I knew was a crock, because I don't think any one of them—his wife, his kids, his mother—gave a shit about his happiness.

Finally, after about a year, John and I broke it off. The pressure got to be too much, for both of us. I was the one who made the decision to call it quits, but I think we were both relieved. We still spoke at the office, and sometimes he'd call me at home just to see how I was. Occasionally, we'd even go out for a friendly drink. That's it.

The last time I saw him was near the end of October. He stopped by my desk to tell me he'd been canned. He asked if I'd cover for him for a couple of weeks while he looked for another job. He wanted me to tell his wife if she called that he couldn't get to the phone and then I was supposed to call his beeper with a code that would tell him to call his wife. I was glad to do it. I felt sorry for him. Things just never seemed to break his way.

No one at the office ever knew about us, so I got no special attention when this happened. I figured I was safe. As it turned out, I was wrong. About a week after the bodies were discovered, I got a visit from some state investigator.

CHAPTER NINE:
AL, THE POSTMAN

After the third time, I got a little suspicious, you know. Once, okay. Twice, maybe. But three times? Well then, unless you're a complete fool, which I'm happy to say I'm not—but hey, don't ask my wife about that, she might disagree—you know there's something fishy going on.

He didn't think I saw him, but I did. He used to wait in his car just beyond the entrance to Oakdale Drive, his street, and then, when I went through, he'd drive in after me, pull alongside my truck and then ask, as innocent as you please, whether there was any mail for him. He'd put it this way, "I'll save you the trouble of putting it in my mailbox, Al." As if that was any more trouble than standing there in the street pulling mail out of order. I'd give him what I had and then watch as he thumbed through it. The first couple times, he didn't even do that. He'd just stuff it in his pocket, get back in his car and drive off. But after that, he didn't bother. Nope. He'd just look through it right there in front of me, like I wasn't even there. He'd pull out what he was looking for and then take the rest and shove it in the mailbox in front of his house.

That he was doing it didn't bother me much—hey, I've seen stranger things in my time—but the way he went about it sure did. He got on my nerves, waiting there for me. He especially got on my nerves when he made some crack like, "A little late this morning, aren't you?"

Who the hell did he think he was? My supervisor? I didn't

63

have to give any explanations to him. I do my job, been doing it nearly thirty years, and I don't need some wise-ass idiot watching me and criticizing my every move. Just who did he think he was? Did he think just because he lived in a ritzy neighborhood he was better than me? No, sir, he wasn't. He didn't have the foggiest idea what went into the job. He didn't know the pressures we're under, the rules we've got to follow. He could just damn well wait for his mail like the rest of us. Once or twice, okay, but a regular habit of it. No, sir. Not on my route.

I'm nobody's fool. I knew what he was looking for. At first, I only suspected. But I could be as sneaky as him so, after the third or fourth time, I made sure I knew just what letters they had that morning and then, after he went through the mail and took out what he wanted and then stuffed the rest back into the box and took off, I checked. I went to that box and I opened it and I pulled out his mail. Just like I thought. Bills. That's what he was after. Every damn one of them was gone. He was hiding them from his wife, that's what he was doing. He didn't want her to know they weren't being paid. Because that's what it was. Those bills were overdue. I'm nobody's fool. No, sir. You got to get up pretty early in the A.M. to pull the wool over these eyes. And nobody gets up earlier than the mailman.

I felt like saying to him, "Why are you waiting and criticizing me? Why not just pay the damn things, like the rest of us?" These rich people, they think they own the world. They think they're better than us. But they're not. They're just like the rest of us, only sometimes worse. Trying to be what they aren't. It's a shame. A damn shame.

One day it just stopped. Got word from the main office that we were to hold all mail because they were going on vacation. That was fine by me. I didn't give a damn whether I ever delivered another piece of mail to that house. It made my life a lot easier. I didn't have to look forward to someone waiting for me to show up. I could sit there an extra five, ten minutes over my coffee and muffin. I do my job, but I don't have to be on any schedule like a railroad, do I?

When I found out what he'd done, it didn't surprise me one bit. I could've told you something like that might happen just from the way he spoke to me, just from his attitude. He didn't have respect for other people. You don't have respect for other people, you're capable of doing just what he did.

Chapter Ten:
Stanley Blake

Let's examine this in terms of a chart, shall we? This chart is to be divided into four distinct bar graphs, each one representing a year, beginning in 2000 and ending in 2005. For the purposes of this illustration, we'll say that 100 is at the top of the chart and zero at the bottom. Now, try to follow me on this, because I don't actually have a visual aid reconstruction here. By the end of 2000, the bar graph stands at a position that scores approximately in the 18th percentile. The next year, that's 2003, it is, shall we say, in the high 80s, very close to the 90th percentile, a definite upswing. By the end of the next year, 2004, the bar graph shows a precipitous drop, down into the neighborhood of the mid to low 50s, not a very reassuring sign. And in the final year, 2005, to be exact, we are all the way down, mired deep in the mid-20s, a rather disturbing, or to be more appropriate, shocking figure.

To put it into words, for the first two years the subject scored quite high on the graph, but subsequently there was a decided and immensely disappointing decline in job performance and productivity.

This chart illustrates better than I can explain the performance of John Hartman in his time working for the company. But what the chart doesn't tell us is his potential. Let me tell you, it was high. I wouldn't have been among those favoring his hiring if I didn't believe that. And, if you'll recall, those first two years on the job were a testament to that fact.

At first, it was the little things. It wasn't so much that he failed to perform what was expected of him, but rather that he failed to take certain initiatives that should have been taken. He began to display a shocking lack of interest in his work. The tasks he was assigned were completed and usually completed successfully but, for the most part, he stopped there. Later, however, this changed for the worse and his performance actually fell off considerably, to the point where it was obvious to all concerned that he was just not into doing the job, cutting the mustard, so to speak. There were certain careless mistakes, errors of omission, even attitude problems. His work reflected an utter lack of concentration and attentiveness.

At a certain point, during the summer and early fall of 2006, I believe, he even began to take days off from work with no apparent reason. These little personal "holidays," as I call them, became more and more frequent, until finally I had to put a stop to it. I called him into my office one day and read him the riot act. I told him that if he didn't shape up we'd have to let him go. I asked if there were any family problems that might explain his performance. He shook his head, no. I asked if there was anything either I or the company might help him with. Again, no. To be frank, I didn't like his attitude. It was rather haughty, arrogant, even disdainful. I thought if I were the one standing in his shoes I might be a little more contrite. But not him. He stood there as if he'd done absolutely nothing wrong, as if I were the culprit for calling him out.

Nothing changed. His performance was still sub-par and the days off from work increased rather than decreased. It was a matter of gross insubordination, almost as if he were flaunting it in our faces. Something had to be done.

The axe finally fell sometime near the early part of October. It pained me, but it was something that had to be done. I tried to do it as gently as possible. There's no such thing at our company as a pink slip. I called him into my office, explained our position, and offered any help I could in finding him another, less taxing position, though certainly not in our organization. He took it well, almost as if he'd been expecting it. Maybe he was. The handwriting had been on the wall for almost a year. In fact, I almost felt as if he were daring us to fire him.

I said there was no hurry. He would get severance, of course, and there would be a nice lump sum from his employee's benefit fund. I even offered to allow him the use of his office for a week as an aid in finding another job. He said that wouldn't be necessary and he thanked me, though for what I can't imagine.

And that was that. Somehow, I just can't help feeling that Hartman, as bright and talented as he was, was in over his head. Another line of work, I thought, might suit him just fine. But with our company, well, he was just in over his head.

CHAPTER ELEVEN:
JAMES KIRKLAND

Just when it looked like things had calmed down and were returning to normal, something else happened that rocked the community.

It was about eight o'clock in the evening, two weeks after the bodies had been discovered. I happened to look out the window and a flash of bright light coming from the Hartman house caught my eye. You know, with the times we're in now, my first thought was some kind of terrorist attack. But who would attack up here?

When I ran outside and looked across the street I could see that the whole damn house was on fire. Flames shot into the air like Fourth of July roman candles, and clumps of thick, black smoke poured from the windows and twisted into the air, blown in several directions at once by the shifting, gusty winds. The fire was so intense, burning with such brightness, that the entire other side of the street looked like it was bathed in sunlight. I could hear the crackling sounds of the fire and the crumbling of the house, which burned as if it were made of cardboard. It was a real humdinger. I went back inside and yelled to my wife to call the fire department, which she did while I grabbed my overcoat and went out on the front lawn to keep an eye on things. Evidently, someone else had phoned in the alarm before us because only a moment or two passed before the fire engines arrived. It was almost an instant replay of the night they found the bodies, only this time there was a real light show.

It took almost three hours to put out the fire, and that was with two other fire trucks from the adjoining townships. By the time it was over all that remained of the Hartman house was a heap of ashes, some smoldering timber, and the blackened, discolored cement foundation. A few nearby trees were completely destroyed by the leaping flames while others, further away, were left with blackened leaves and scorched limbs. The front lawn was a virtual swamp from the water used to put out the fire. It was nothing but mud and brown, burnt-out grass.

Now there was only a big, gaping, ugly hole across the street where the Hartman house used to be.

The next day, rumors ran rampant. The most prevalent theory was that Hartman had returned and set fire to the house. That there was some kind of evidence the cops had missed that he wanted to get rid of. Sort of the final act in his horrendous crime spree. Ridiculous, of course, because why would he risk coming back, especially since everyone knew he was the murderer. Others, mostly kids in the neighborhood, their imaginations fueled by Hollywood films and post-Halloween fantasies, attributed the fire to the ghosts of the Hartman family, laying the conflagration directly at the hands of the old woman, whom they naturally began referring to as a witch. Still others subscribed to the theory that the fire was probably accidental, the result of paint-soaked rags in the basement. But this supposition was quickly proved wrong by fire officials who, after first calling it suspicious in origin, finally declared it arson.

My wife, like so many others, was convinced Hartman had returned and, frankly, she was scared to death. She couldn't sleep for several nights afterward. She even talked about moving away, which was absolutely crazy.

"Why in heaven's name would he come back?" I asked.

"Why did he kill his family? Does he need a reason for anything he does from now on?"

"Okay, so let's say he's alive and he did come back and set fire to his own house. It's done now, so what is there to worry about? He'd never come back. He wouldn't risk it. Do you think he's out to depopulate the entire town of Sedgewick? Does that sound reasonable to you?"

"If he risked it once, he'd do it again," she said, and no amount of logic could change her mind. She wasn't alone in her belief. Some people kicked around the idea of hiring an armed guard to patrol the area. Fortunately, that idea came to nothing because if it had happened it would have been like living in an armed camp. Or worse, like living in New York City.

I figured the fire was either set by a bunch of kids looking for kicks, or by someone who wanted to erase the whole terrible incident from everyone's mind and thought the best way to do that would be to make the house just disappear. Or maybe it was just a case of spontaneous combustion—you know, it happens.

Every time I walked by I had to avert my eyes because instead of letting people forget about the Hartman murders, the fire and its aftermath just called attention to them. Finally, a few days after the fire, those of us on the block couldn't stand it anymore, so we had a meeting to decide what to do. I was selected to contact the proper authorities to see about some kind of clean-up. I found that Hartman had several mortgages on the property and now, by default, it belonged to the local bank, which was planning to auction it off.

This was good news, though we weren't quite sure as to the type of buyer it might attract. We didn't want some curiosity-seeker purchasing it to make it into some kind of amusement park, nor did we want the value of the property to decrease because of what happened. So, in order to guard against that possibility, several of us got together and established a kind of consortium so that if we didn't approve of the people who were bidding on the property, we could buy it ourselves and then either resell it or, after landscaping the grounds, simply let it lie fallow for a while.

Fortunately, the property was purchased by a well-established Sedgewick family who planned to build a new house and then give it to their daughter as a wedding gift.

So, after all that, it turned out there was nothing to worry about. Nothing, that is, unless you were one of those, like my wife, who believed John Hartman really had returned and torched the place. I admit, the idea was kind of creepy. But I, for one, didn't believe it was very likely.

CHAPTER TWELVE:
REVEREND CHAPMAN

One day, completely out of the blue, as I sat at my desk doodling squares within squares on my blotter and daydreaming about my upcoming vacation—yes, we actually get vacations—I suddenly recalled a conversation I'd had with John Hartman shortly before he disappeared. I was somewhat surprised because I thought by that time I'd been able to exorcise John and all thoughts of him from my mind. But obviously, I was wrong.

I was on my way to the local drugstore to fill a prescription for my daughter, who'd come down with some sort of intestinal virus. I'd just pulled into a parking spot as John came out of the store, headed toward his car. Though there was an early fall nip in the air, the sky was bright and cloudless and I remember thinking he was a bit overdressed, wearing a beige racing cap and black trench coat with the collar turned up. His head was down, his shoulders hunched forward, as if protecting himself from a nonexistent wind. He seemed preoccupied and probably would have walked right past me if I hadn't called out his name. As he looked up to see who it was, he appeared to be a little disoriented, as if he'd just been awakened from a deep sleep.

"Oh, hello, Reverend," he said softly as he put what I believe was a small pharmacy package into his coat pocket.

"How are you, John?"

"Fine," he replied, his eyes darting to either side of me, then stopping at a point somewhere just below my chin, where they remained for the rest of our conversation.

"You look a little tired," I remarked, noting the dark circles under his eyes and a drawn, haggard look on his face.

"I've been . . . busy," he said, his hands jammed into his trench coat pockets as if protecting something very valuable.

"Work?"

"Uh-huh."

"On Sundays, too?" I said with a smile, because I was pulling his leg.

"Sunday?" he repeated. "Oh . . . yes . . . Sundays. Well, not work actually. Uh . . . family . . . uh . . . matters."

He seemed nervous, so I put my hand on his shoulder in a friendly gesture, but he shuddered and then shrank under my touch, so I pulled back immediately. "I'm only teasing, John. You don't owe me any explanation. Are you all right?"

"I'm fine."

"You're sure?"

"Yes, I'm sure," he replied. Though he was standing in one spot, he couldn't seem to remain still. He kept shifting his weight from one foot to the other, and his body seemed to twitch uncontrollably beneath his trench coat. He looked pale, which was why I asked how he was.

"Well, you seem to be in a bit of a fog today. How's the family? Everything all right at home?"

He hesitated a moment. "They're fine. Into their own things. Friends, school, work, you know how things are, Reverend."

"Of course. Am I keeping you from something, John?"

"No. I . . . I was just picking up some things for the house."

"Haven't seen you around much lately, John. We could sure use your help in Sunday school. We're a little shorthanded."

"I've been to the city a lot lately." He raised his head, as if to see if I was still there. Then, quickly, he dropped it again. "Not New Haven. New York."

"Seeing the sights?"

"Yes. The sights." His voice trailed off and then, almost as an afterthought, he added, "You know, Reverend, I saw something very odd down there the other day. Something you might be interested in. I was walking past the Plaza Hotel and I saw this fellow standing there and on a chair next to him was one of those ventriloquist's dummies. Only this one was black and he . . . it . . . was wearing a plaid shirt, camel's hair vest and cap, kind of like the one I'm wearing now. And in front of them there was this hand-printed sign that said, 'Jesus speaks through the dummy.'

"I hung around for a couple of minutes, waiting for something to happen, but nothing did. He just stood there, leaning against the building, drinking a cup of coffee, not saying anything, just looking kind of bored, while the dummy just sat there, its mouth hanging open. I wanted to stick around a little longer, just to see if something was going to happen, but I had to go. I suppose the guy was on a break, but you know, I really wanted to hear what that dummy had to say. I was just curious, is all. A couple days later I was back in the city and I went back to the same spot, but the dummy wasn't there. I hung around for a while, on the off chance he might come back, but he never did. So what do you make of that, Reverend?"

I was speechless. What could I say? I wasn't even sure John was serious. How could he be? But still, the way he told it and all, with such sincerity, I honestly couldn't be sure. So I simply shrugged and said, "The city is full of weirdoes, John. I'm sure it was just another scheme to get people's money."

He looked hurt, as if by not taking his story seriously I was somehow casting aspersions on him, that I wasn't taking him seriously enough. And yet, because not once during our conversation did he ever look me directly in the eye, could I be absolutely sure he wasn't pulling my leg. Like I said before, with John I was never quite sure whether he was testing me or not.

After all, what could be more patently ridiculous than Jesus speaking through a black dummy in front of the Plaza Hotel?

Chapter Thirteen:
Charlie Floyd

This Hartman guy was a real scumbag. I know. I know. Murderers. Scumbags. They should be synonymous. But that's not always the case. Some of the most likable people I've met were murderers. And charming, too. Likability and violence aren't always contradictory. But the more I learned about Hartman, the less I liked him. He was arrogant, anti-social and pretentious. A two-faced intellectual snob who cheated on his wife and then, when things started to go sour, pulled the plug on his whole family. And so far as I could tell, without a wisp of conscience or a moment of remorse, which ruled out any possibility we were dealing with anything but a cold-blooded killer, an out-and-out sociopath. Like I said, a real scumbag.

Some people think Hartman's dead. That he offed himself. That we'll never find him. Not me. He's alive, all right. I feel it in my gut. I know this sounds spooky, mystical even, but I can actually feel his earthly presence, his evil is still among us. He's still out there, sure enough, just waiting for me to find him. And I will. Because there's nothing I want more. Nothing. I've been so wound up I can't sleep at night. Listen, I even carry this photo we found of him—taken maybe ten years ago—with me all the time. We got it from his sister, because he destroyed all the others in the house. I study it like a Dashing Dan studies commuter train schedules. I even keep it right out on the night table next to me while I sleep. It isn't much, but it's all we have: a full-body shot of him dressed in summer attire, a short-sleeved shirt and light-colored casual slacks, standing in front of his house in Syracuse, with a half-coiled hose in his hand, the nozzle pointed down toward the ground and a small puddle of water at his feet. We had it blown up so just his faced showed. A nearby tree cast a slight shadow over him, but his face was still visible, a face remarkably lacking in any emotion. No expression whatsoever, as if he was completely unaware of having his picture taken. Just a moment frozen in time.

I look at that photo so often you'd think I'd know his face by heart, yet somehow it eludes me. And so, every so often during the day, I whip it out and study it, trying to memorize each and every centimeter, like a child trying to memorize his multiplication tables. But an hour later it's gone and so I have to look at it again. It's that kind of face. Totally unmemorable. Try as I might, I can't seem to get it to stay with me, though I know it's a face I'd recognize immediately if I ever saw it in real life, which was just what I had in mind. It's funny but at night, with the lights out and me lying in bed unable to sleep, that face becomes clearer, sharper. And sometimes, after falling asleep, I wake suddenly, see the face in front of me, then quickly turn on the light and grab the photo just to make sure it's the same face.

You might say I'm obsessed. I like to think of it as focused. Like anyone who's good at his job.

To give the bastard his due, it wasn't going to be easy to find him. He gave himself plenty of time to disappear and he'd covered his tracks real good. It also looked as if he made damn sure he had more than enough dough to see him through for a while. After all, we found nothing of value in the house, except for two practically worthless rings on his mother's finger, the kind that have sentimental value maybe, and a gold wedding band on his wife's hand. That was it. And the bank accounts were bone dry.

So tell me the killings weren't planned. Tell me it was the work of a deranged psycho. Yeah, tell me that, and then tell me another one.

It wasn't tough finding the woman he was fooling around with. How did I know there was someone? There always is, that's how. It was simply a matter of finding her. And the best place to start was where he worked, because I didn't think he was the type to pick up skirts in a bar.

I went to his office and questioned everyone, and the more I questioned the more obvious it became who it was. Believe me, in an office situation there are very few secrets. You may think there are, but you'd only be kidding yourself. What else have people to do with their time but watch other people slip on banana peels and then gossip about them?

And yet the woman actually seemed surprised when I confronted her. But she didn't deny it.

"Okay," she said in a half-whisper, "so you know about us. So what? It's been a long time now. I don't know anything that can possibly help you. I'd tell you if I did . . . just to be over with the whole damn thing. Not that I think that'll ever happen."

"I didn't say you knew anything."

"Then what do you want from me?" she asked, her hands resting on her hips, staring me dead in the eyes with one of the coldest damn looks I'd ever seen, and I've seen plenty of them. It was as if she'd suddenly found a focus for all her hatred, fear and frustration. But that was okay. Sometimes, I can turn that to my advantage.

She was good-looking. About five-six, with sandy-colored, shoulder-length hair that she kept nervously sweeping away from her face. She had beautiful bone structure, though her nose was maybe a little too long for her face. She came on as kind of cocky, but I thought it was all an act. I could tell she was scared. I knew it by her body language. That's something you learn in this business. It's not only about the face . . . and the eyes. In fact, it's often the rest of the body that betrays you. She was scared of me. Scared of John Hartman. Maybe even scared of herself. I felt sorry for her. She was a victim, too. Every waking minute she'd have to deal with the fact that she'd been involved with a monster like Hartman. That for various moments in their lives they were a part of each other. She would continually question herself as to what it was in her that was attracted to him. That dark place that needed someone like him to fill. It had to be frightening, a terrible burden to bear. So I felt sorry for her. But still, I had a job to do. And my sympathy for her wasn't going to stop me.

"I'd just like to talk to you. It's important I know everything, from the first moment you met him till the last. I'm going to get to know him as well as you did, better even. That's the only way I'll catch him."

"I don't give a shit if you catch him."

"Sure you do. But even if you don't, I don't give a shit about that. I don't need you standing on the sidelines rooting me on. But the fact is, you'll help. Whether you want to or not."

She was quiet. Sizing me up. She squeezed her hands together nervously. Her eyes darted back and forth. She wet her lips. I sat tight. The less I said, the more I'd get from her. Eventually, she, not me, would fill the silence. In fact, I could see that in a strange way the idea actually appealed to her, but she was fighting it. Maybe she thought talking to me was a way to rid herself of the demons. And maybe it was.

"Okay. I'll talk to you. But not here."

"I can understand that."

She bit her lower lip. "And not at the police station, either."

"I can understand that, too. You have a favorite bar or something?"

80

Her face hardened. "What kind of woman do you think I am?"

"I don't know," I said, "but I suppose I'm going to find out. Someplace else? Somewhere you'll feel comfortable. Your place, maybe?"

"I don't know if I want someone like you in my home," she said, and she wasn't smiling.

"You've had worse," I shot back, but as soon as I said it I was sorry. I had every right to judge Hartman for what he'd done, but not her. Sometimes, the trouble with this job is that you tend to judge people by standards no one could possibly live up to. It's a nasty habit and, when I do it, I don't like myself too much. Unfortunately, cynicism goes with the job and even more unfortunately it often spills into your personal life, fucking up relationships that are important. So, I admit it, I'm cynical. But it's not something I take any particular pride in. It's just the way things are.

"I'm sorry," I mumbled. "I know that sounded pretty bad."

She turned away and, with her back to me said, "Tonight. Eight o'clock. And I'm sure you've got the address."

CHAPTER FOURTEEN:
CHRISTOPHER JACKSON

He was in my class at school, but we didn't hang out or anything. You know, like we were buds or anything like that. If you wanna know the truth, he was kind of a jerk, Paul, I mean. He came off like this really nice guy, but when you got to know him he wasn't all that nice.

He was a real wise-ass, you know. And he was always doing stupid things, like . . . well, like once a bunch of us went to this store in town and he thought it was like cool to like steal stuff. You know, not even stuff that was like worth anything. Like a magazine, or some candy. That's what he'd take. And he, like, smoked. And I think he like drank and like did drugs, too. Once, he brought a bottle of beer to school in his knapsack and during lunch he made sure that everyone saw it. Like it made him a big man or something. And he was always bragging about what he got away with when he was back in Syracuse. And he was always putting down everyone, like they weren't as smart as him or as cool as him. And like, the truth is, he wasn't cool at all. He was kind of a nerd, actually. He was always talking about what he was going to do to this girl or that girl, but we didn't think he'd even ever had a date. I mean, I never even saw him talking to a girl or anything. He would just talk about it, like we were supposed to be impressed or something. But we weren't impressed. We just thought it was, like an idiot.

And he never let anyone go over to his house, not that we wanted to or anything. He was just like weird, you know. We always used to joke that if anyone came into the school and shot it up, like they did at that place Columbine, it would be Paul. At least that's what we thought . . . not that I'm saying he'd actually do it or anything.

But no one ever pushed him around or anything. Maybe that's because he had an older brother and we'd heard some stuff about him. That he was really tough. Paul said he was a black belt and that up in Syracuse he'd spent some time in juvie because he beat up a kid. But we didn't really believe that. We thought that was just Paul talking, you know. But we didn't want to take any chances. Because, you know, this time he might be telling the truth.

You know, kids like Paul, they're not cool. They're just pathetic.

Chapter Fifteen:
Jerry Kovacs

If John Hartman had a friend, I guess I was it.

I don't mean to say he was some kind of obnoxious jerk who couldn't make or maintain friendships, it's just that he didn't go out of his way to make a lot of friends. So, like I said, if John Hartman had a best friend, I guess I was it.

We met in Syracuse in the late '80s. We worked for the same company. In fact, we pretty much had the same job. We had other things in common, too. Neither of us was originally from upstate New York. He was a real sports nut and so was I. He had kids, so did I. He had a wife who hated Syracuse, so did I.

We used to have drinks together sometimes after work. And we'd go to S.U. games whenever we could manage to sneak off. Jeez, we were like two little kids playing hooky from school. And let me tell you, John loved it. It was like he was getting away with something. And I guess he was. He was getting away from a wife who gave him all kinds of shit, a mother who put him down whenever she got the chance, and kids who were pretty much out of control, at least once they were outside the house. In short, he was getting away from a life that was pulling him under.

He loved going to those games. But there's a funny thing about that. He never rooted for S.U. Always for the visiting team, no matter who it was, even Penn State or Pitt, our arch-rivals. I never understood that. I asked him about it once. He shrugged, as if he'd never given it a second thought, and said,

"I guess I just like to be contrary."

I said, "What's that supposed to mean?"

"Well, everybody else in this place is wearing orange, so I don't suppose one more would make a difference. I want to make a difference. I don't want to be part of thousands of winners. But if the other team wins, that's something else, isn't it? Then I'll be one of the few winners here, won't I?"

I didn't answer. I just figured John was just one of those people who identified with the underdog. But now, thinking back, maybe it was more than that. Maybe he just hated the fact that the home team had all those rooters yelling for their success. I don't think he really wanted to see any of us going home happy. He wasn't going home happy, so why should we?

Basically, he wasn't happy because of two things: his job and his family. Let me explain.

His wife was the kind of woman who was never happy and she had to make sure that no around her was either. I can honestly say that I never, ever saw her crack a smile. Not that I saw her that much, you understand. Because she kind of kept to herself. She was a hypochondriac, always complaining about some ache or pain. She even told some folks that she was diagnosed with breast cancer, but John said that wasn't true. She'd had a small lump, but it was benign. Nothing to worry about, he said. But she liked attention, so she blew it up into something serious. And there's nothing more serious than cancer. She was also someone who always found fault, no matter how small or insignificant it might be. For the last year John was in Syracuse her harping took the form of relentlessly telling him how much she hated the place. She never let up. John told me she despised the city itself, which she said was gray and dingy and depressing. She also hated the weather, which was snowy and cold in the winter, really hot in the summer, and cloudy all the time. She hated the people, too, who she said were provincial and had little or nothing to offer in the way of any intellectual stimulation or sophistication. It was, she said, basically just another overgrown university town and, as a result, she and John and the rest of the family were simply another anonymous family of "townies" to be looked down on. And, of course, she hated the company he worked for, which, she said, didn't appreciate him. She was always telling him to ask for more money and threatened to leave if he didn't get it. John was a pragmatist. He didn't like his job either, but he knew he needed to work to support his family and that jobs were pretty scarce, what with the economy tanking after 9/11.

I only met Adele a couple of times. Like I said, she didn't go out much and I don't think she thought much of my wife and me. Maybe she was jealous of our friendship, John and me, or maybe she just didn't want anything or anyone to interfere with her crusade to get out of Syracuse. Or maybe she just thought we were beneath her. Most likely, all of the above.

One day, a recruiter from Xerox showed up at the office looking for talent to spirit away to Connecticut. John was a prime target. But he was conflicted. One side wanted the job because it would mean he could give his wife and mother what they wanted. Another side didn't want the job because it represented another obstacle. What I mean is that John hated what he was doing and taking that job would be another sign that he was trapped in corporate America.

But he went after the job just the same. Maybe it was guilt because he felt responsible for taking his family away from Chicago and moving them to Syracuse where they spent eight months of the year digging out from under snowdrifts high enough to hide a small tree. By this time his wife had slipped into fits of depression and John was worried. If he'd asked me, I would have told him they were a sham, just a form of manipulation. But John fell for it.

So he put in his bid and he told me that the night he told his wife she was ecstatic. She hugged him and told him how terrific it would be. He tried to calm her down, telling her he'd only applied for the job, not gotten it, but she wasn't listening. She just wanted out and she was sure this was the ticket, all of which just put more pressure on him.

"I shouldn't have mentioned it to her, Jerry," he said.

"Loose lips sink ships."

"I know, but what's done is done. I've got to get that job now or my life won't be worth shit. Already Adele is making a detailed list of all the things that have to be done before we can move, everything from selling the damn house to hiring the right moving company. She can be very thorough when she puts her mind to it. Very single-minded, too. She even tried to pin me down as to how much they'll offer."

"What'd you tell her?"

"I told her I didn't think it would be much more than what I was making here. She didn't believe me. She said, 'John, we're talking about a big company. One of the Fortune 500.' I couldn't reason with her. She didn't want to listen."

I knew John was a shoo-in, especially when they asked him down to Connecticut to meet with some of the top execs. He went, but he wasn't happy about it. I think he really wanted to be turned down. After he came back he confided to me that he'd gotten the job. But he hadn't told anybody else. I think he was toying with the idea of lying about it. That's what I think. But in the end, either he didn't have the guts or he was too moral to lie. And yeah, there was another thing, too. I think John was afraid that if he didn't get the job it would send his wife over the edge. I knew she was a lot stronger than that, but I don't think John did.

They wanted him to start in March. She wanted to move right away. He argued against it. He didn't want to take the kids out of school in the middle of the semester. The company had offered to put him up in a hotel until he found a house and fly him back to Syracuse weekends to spend with the family. Eventually, he convinced Adele that's what they ought to do. It wasn't easy, though, and a slight modification was made: she was to fly down to Connecticut weekends until they found a house.

In late April, John was back for a weekend and we had a drink. He didn't look good. Something was bothering him. He wasn't the type to open up easily, but, after some prodding and a couple beers, he finally told me what it was.

"Adele found the house she wants."

"So?"

"It's nineteen rooms. Jerry, we need a nineteen-room house like I need my own Lear jet."

"Nice but superfluous, huh?"

"You got it. But she fell in love with it. She calls it her dream house."

"And your nightmare, huh?"

"I tried to tell her it's much more than we need and that it'll be hell to keep up, not to mention that it's way out of our price range. It's too near the water. We need something inland, something cheaper. She told me I think too small. She says we're on the way up and we need something apropos. To her, life is all style and very little substance. And then she started pitching the practicality to me."

"Practicality."

"Yeah. Each kid can have his own room. My mother can have hers. And we can have friends stay over."

"What friends are those, John? Have you been keeping something from me?"

"Well, she doesn't mean you and Joan. That's for sure."

"Big surprise. Are these maybe some imaginary playmates she has?"

"She figures to make friends down there."

"Yeah, well, good luck to her."

"I'm worried about money. I don't think we can swing it. She says to look at it as an investment, and I guess she's not wrong, but I don't know. It's quite a lot to take on."

"John, I'm going to give you some advice. I know you're not going to take it, but I'll give it anyway. That way, when you come to me down the road I can give you one of those 'I told you so,' looks. Don't do it. It's one more obligation you don't need."

But, of course, he eventually talked himself into it. The investment, the much-needed room, made it worth it. He said, "I can lose myself in all that space when I want to. I'll have all the solitude I need. Nineteen rooms. 'Thus let me live, unseen, unknown;/Thus unlamented let me die,' " he said.

I thought that last bit a little morbid, but I didn't say anything. What was the use? He'd already made up his mind. He was doing what he thought was right, so who was I to make trouble? Frankly, I hoped I was wrong, that everything would work out. Well, it didn't, did it?

For the first year while he was down there he used to call every couple weeks. He'd tell me how terrific things were and I believed him. Why shouldn't I? After a while, I stopped hearing from him. I'd call. Sometimes he'd talk. Other times I'd leave a message, but he never returned my call. After a year or so, I gave up. I figured he didn't want to have anything to do with me, so why strain myself?

Two years ago, I got a job with Xerox and was transferred down to Connecticut. I took a shot. I called John at his office. He happened to be in and he actually sounded pleased I was moving down. He even offered to put me up till we found a place. I said, "John, maybe you ought to check with Adele first." He said, "Don't be ridiculous. I don't have to check with anybody. We have plenty of room—remember?" "Okay," I said, "but just do me a favor and ask." He called back the next day and was very apologetic. He said he'd forgotten that the place was being painted. I said I understood. Really, he said, Adele had nothing to do with it. "I believe you, John," I said.

When we moved down a few months later we found a place a couple of towns away, much closer to the office than where John lived. He had us over to dinner and surprisingly, Adele couldn't have been nicer. I couldn't help noticing that the place hadn't been painted, but it sure needed it. I didn't say anything to John. There was no need to embarrass him.

We had lunch a couple times, and he seemed especially gloomy, as if he were in a constant state of pain. I asked him what was wrong, but he never came out and said it. But I do remember he once said, "Ever tried? Ever failed? No matter. Try again. Fail again. Fail better." I asked him where that was from and he said, "It's Samuel Beckett. Worstward Ho!" And then he laughed.

The closest he'd come to actually complaining had to do with the house. I think it became a symbol of everything that was wrong with his life. He told me it was sucking up cash like a vacuum cleaner, bleeding him dry. "We don't even have enough furniture to fill it," he said, and then he told me they'd been forced to take out another mortgage just to keep their heads above water. "It seems every time I turn around something else is going wrong," he said. "The boiler blew, the basement flooded, the cesspool overflowed, the ceiling needs reinforcement, the roof needs to be fixed, the house has to be re-sided, re-winterized, re-caulked and re-painted. Jerry, I'm be-ing re-ed to death. It's too hot in the summer and too cold in the winter. It's a monkey on my back. It's an unwanted member of my family, an albatross around my neck. I hate it. From the minute we moved in my life has been hell."

I didn't have the heart to tell him that to me, his life was hell long before he moved into that house.

I'm not so sure he meant to kill his family as much as he did that house—and when it burned down, well, I'm not saying John had anything to do with that, but I am sure, if he's still alive, he'd be smiling about it.

Why do I think he did it? I don't know. When something like this happens you try to go back over the time you spent with the person and pick up clues, reasons why it might happen. But memory plays tricks on you. I think if you examine anyone's life closely enough you can come up with a whole bunch of reasons, some of them logical, others not, why someone does a particular thing. In the end, though, you never really know because it's impossible to get into somebody else's head, or experience what they're experiencing or feel what they're feeling. All I know is, John was not a happy camper and my guess is he still isn't happy . . . if he's alive, that is.

I wouldn't say I really knew him. I spent time with him, sure, and we spoke about some personal things, though I always felt he was holding back, but we were never what you'd call close. I wish I could have helped him. I wish he was the kind of guy who'd come for advice or talk things out, but he wasn't. He held things in and he let them stew. If you ask me, the top finally blew.

John was a likable fellow when you got to know him. Strange, but likable. As a matter of fact, if I saw him tomorrow, I'd probably just sit down with him and start talking about the Knicks or the Giants.

But then, he's probably not the same guy I knew up in Syracuse, right? No, I guess one night last November changed all that.

CHAPTER SIXTEEN:
JOSEPH SCHLITZ

I'm a licensed private investigator, working out of New Haven, Connecticut. My name is Joseph Schlitz. No joke. And no relation. I get more than my share of ribbing about that. No need to explain why, right?

In the late spring of 2000, I was employed by Adele Hartman to keep an eye on her husband. Nothing peculiar about that. She suspected him of adultery and hired me to find out for sure. She didn't want pictures. She just wanted to know. Ignorance is bliss to some people, not to others. Me, I like to know everything about everybody. That's probably why I'm in the business I'm in. I get paid for being nosy.

I kept a pretty comprehensive log while I followed John Hartman, on and off, for a month and a half, commencing in mid-May and ending just after July 4. Because that's what I do. I'm a very thorough man. I've found that it usually pays off. By the time I'm finished I know more about the person I'm checking out than he—or she, because sometimes it's a woman I'm hired to check out—knows about himself.

It didn't take me that long to find out that John Hartman had a little something on the side. When I went to Mrs. Hartman to report my findings, she asked me to stay on the case. I didn't ask why, because I didn't care. It wasn't my business. She paid on time, in cash, and the work was easy. That's all I cared about. Look, I've got a family of my own to support.

Someone wants to throw good money after bad, that's fine with me.

When I told her what I found out, she didn't rant or rave or break down in tears. Instead, her eyes kinda narrowed and she said, "Thank you," as if I'd just held the door open for her. I didn't think that was particularly odd, though. After all, if someone goes to all the trouble of hiring a private detective to follow her husband, believe me, she already knows there's some hanky-panky going on. Usually, they just want to know who, or the gory details, or they want hard evidence for the divorce so they can take their spouse to the cleaners. But I don't think that was the case here. If she'd just wanted evidence for the lawyers, she already had more than enough. I think it was just a matter of curiosity or else maybe she planned to give him some kind of ultimatum and wanted to be sure he gave up the other woman. Another reason people take that kind of news calmly is because they're ashamed. They take it as a reflection on themselves, like they're to blame, and they're embarrassed about it. It's like they don't want to admit, even to a stranger, that in some way they've been inadequate, though that's not necessarily the case. Still, that's the way they take it. But then they usually just pay me off and never want to see me again. They don't want me hanging around, like she did. That baffled me a little, but to tell you the truth, I didn't lose much sleep over it.

After I made my report, that's when she asked me to stay on the case. Our arrangement was this: I wasn't to follow him all the time, just when she called and asked me to, which turned out to be a couple times a week. I don't know why she wanted it that way, but she did. I was happy to oblige.

Like I said, I was let go right after July 4. A couple days before, I got a call from Mrs. Hartman. She said her husband was planning on taking the three kids down to the city to watch the festivities and wanted to know if I was available to follow them. I asked why she didn't go herself. She said she was sick. How about her mother-in-law, which would be a lot cheaper than hiring me? No. She had bad feet and couldn't stand. I told her I didn't think anything untoward would happen while the kids were along, but she was adamant, so I said to myself, "Don't fight it, Joe. Go with the flow."

Quarter to eight, I parked across from the Hartman house, about twenty feet or so down the road past their yard, and waited. If anyone asked, I was a friend of John's. We were going down to the city together.

It was a beautiful day. Bright and clear, with a slight breeze coming in off the Sound. About 8:15, Hartman came out of the house. He seemed agitated. He walked around the yard, every so often stooping down to pick up a weed or a few blades of grass, then tossing them in the air. He looked like he was talking to himself. A couple minutes later, his youngest son, Paul, came out and spoke to him. It got a little heated. Maybe Hartman had changed his mind about going down to the city and the kid was trying to talk him back into it. Or maybe the kid was just giving him some lip. I might be exaggerating a little, but I wouldn't have been surprised if they'd come to blows.

Hartman went back into the house and a few minutes later they all came straggling out, like going with him was the last thing they wanted to do. They were about to get into the car when Hartman sent one of the kids—the girl—back into the house. A minute later, she came back with an armful of brown sandwich bags, their lunches. When everything was stowed in the trunk, they were off, with me tailing behind at a respectable distance, until we reached the thruway. Once on the open road, I moved back and forth, following a while, then leading a while, occasionally even pulling up alongside them. The kids were laughing and having a good time, but Hartman just stared straight ahead, his face frozen.

They parked off Broadway, in the eighties. I pulled up ahead and parked between West End and Riverside, then waited for them to walk by. They were going to the river, to watch the ships. Once we crossed Riverside, the crowds thickened and I had to be careful not to lose them. It occurred to me that this might be a good place for a rendezvous. Maybe the Mrs. wasn't as far off base as I'd thought.

It didn't take long for them to find a spot on the river bank. Now and then a firecracker exploded somewhere behind us and a cheer would go up. Some folks had already staked out blankets along the edge of the water and were eating picnic lunches while radios, some as large as suitcases, blasted a curious mix of patriotic, rock and salsa music. Hartman just stood there impassively, through it all. I got closer. Soon, I was no more than a couple of feet from him, the closest I'd ever been, actually. He was smaller than I'd thought. He was several feet behind his kids, who were waving at the passing boats and tossing small pebbles into the water. I was studying his face and saw this real panicky look. He became very agitated and slowly he began to back away. Uh-oh, I thought, here it comes. And I was ready to take after him. But it was more like he was confused because he wasn't going anywhere in particular. He just wandered off, away from the crowd.

His oldest son, Edward, saw his father move away and said, "Hey, Dad, where you going?"

"What?" Hartman said, looking totally bewildered.

"Where you going?"

"Uh, the wind," Hartman stammered. "My hair's getting messed. I thought I'd go back to the car and get my hat."

"Hey, Dad, I hate to tell you, but there isn't that much to blow around anymore," his kid cracked.

Hartman, looking like a beaten man, inched forward, but I

could tell by the look on his face that his kid's crack had stung. I sympathized. None of us like to be reminded we're getting old, especially by our kids. I don't mind telling you, I felt like going over there and smacking the kid myself. Fuckin' wise-ass.

Later, there was a to-do about lunch. The sandwiches had been left back in the car, purposely Hartman thought, and the kids didn't want to go back and get them. So they wound up buying hotdogs and stuff. Only Hartman didn't seem to have enough cash on him, so the kids, who razzed him about it, had to chip in. I was embarrassed for him. He'd probably just walked out without enough dough in his pocket. Happens to me all the time. Thank God for ATMs.

When it got to be around four o'clock, I moved in and, since I was kind of curious as to what kind of fellow he was, I struck up a conversation. I mean, I kinda felt like I knew the guy already, what with all the time we'd spent "together." I knew it might make it rough for me in the future, but I wasn't thinking about that. I just wanted to have some kind of actual contact with him. Up to then, he'd just been a car or a suit to me. I wanted to see what he was really like.

"Some day, huh?"

He didn't answer. I wasn't sure he heard me, so I repeated it.

"Are you talking to me?" he asked.

"Yeah, it's really something, isn't it?"

". . . I suppose."

"Makes you kinda proud to be an American, don't it?"

"Really?"

"Sure. I mean, I'm a grown man, but I still get a rush from something like this. Especially after all that 9/11 stuff a few years ago."

"You think everyone's happy here?"

"Here where?"

"Here. In this country. In this city. Here."

"Of course not. All I'm saying is it's good to be alive on a day like this. Something like this makes you think things can be better, right?"

"I'm not so sure about that," he muttered.

"You're not worried about that terrorist thing, are you?"

He shook his head.

"I mean, it is something to worry about, right? They hit us once, they could hit us again. That's why we have to be prepared, right? That's why we had to go in there and take care of them. Before they have a chance to do it again. Don't you agree?"

"I don't know . . . I guess it's good to be . . . prepared."

"Well, look, everybody's got problems, but on a day like this, I don't know, I guess it makes it a little easier to forget them, at least for a while."

He shook his head. "Not for me."

"Why's that?"

"Just reminds me of everything that's wrong with my life."

"Like what, if you don't mind my asking?"

I don't know why I asked. I guess I was just curious, is all, as to what could possibly be wrong in a man's life who seemed to have everything. Certainly more than me. Nice house, nice kids, a wife, a mistress. I mean, if he was down in the dumps, what chance was there for a guy like me?

He sighed. "I'm a . . . failure."

"What's that mean, a failure? I don't know you from Adam, pal, but you don't look like a failure to me."

"I . . . I . . . am. I've let my . . . family . . . down . . ."

"How's that?" I asked, but he never answered me. Instead, he said, "I've got to go now. Sorry." He went over to his kids and herded them back to the car, as I followed, losing myself in the crowd.

A couple hours later, we were back in Sedgewick. I parked at the end of the block to jot down some notes. As far as I was concerned, I was finished for the day. But a moment later, I heard the Hartmans' front door open and shut. I looked over my shoulder just in time to see Hartman get into his car, slam the door, then drive off. Though technically I was off-duty, I followed him anyway. Mostly because I was curious. Turned out he wound up at the apartment of the other woman, a gal named Janie McClellan.

The next day, I delivered what turned out to be my final report to Mrs. Hartman over the phone. I told her nothing out of the ordinary had happened in the city. I didn't say anything about what Hartman did after he left the house that night. I don't know why. Maybe I felt sorry for the guy. Besides, what good would it have done to tell her? She already knew. I figure they had some kind of fight and he took off in a huff. Where did she think he'd gone?

Two days later, I got a cashier's check in the mail with a handwritten note that said, simply, "Your services are no longer required." No thanks. Nothing.

So, as far as I was concerned, that was the end of it.

CHAPTER SEVENTEEN:
JUDY HARTMAN SWANSON

Sometimes, when we were kids, I felt sorry for John. I took advantage of the situation plenty, but I felt sorry for him just the same. He was the oldest and the only boy, so big things were expected of him. And I guess there was a lot of pressure on him to perform. He got good grades in school, but Mom and Dad were always on him to do better. Dad wasn't all that successful and so all that drive to succeed was funneled into John. What do the shrinks call it? Projection, right? Well, anyway, John always wanted to be an artist, but there was no way Mom and Dad were going to stand for that. Lawyer. Doctor. Business-man. Those were the alternatives, and John wasn't the type to rebel. I was the rebellious one and, because of that, I got away with murder. Oh, shit, did I really say that? I'm so embarrassed. It seems like I'm treating this like a joke. And I'm not. I'm really not. Really.

Anyway, John looked sad all the time, like he was always on the verge of tears. But he didn't cry and he never complained. He did whatever he was told and he tried so hard to please. A little too hard, if you ask me. Sometimes, it was painful to watch. He had such an incredible sense of responsibility. It used to absolutely kill him if he let somebody down. Even the possibil-ity that he might disappoint someone upset the heck out of him. It's funny, but I don't think of John as ever having been a kid. I've tried, but I just don't see him that way. He was an adult even when he was only five or six years old. He just gave off those mature vibes.

So, I got off easy, since the focus was always on him. Less was expected of me, so whenever I did something that was the least bit out of the ordinary, like maybe getting a B on a quiz—big deal, right?—or something even more insignificant, I was praised to the rafters. If I had been John, I suppose I would have resented me, and maybe he did. Maybe he would have killed me, too, if I'd been in the house that day. But he never raised a hand to me, though I couldn't say the same for me. John accepted his lot and that was that.

At night, I remember John used to go up to the attic to be alone. I don't think he knew that anyone knew he was up there, but I did. Sometimes, I'd go up there in the morning, when he'd left for the day, and find little scraps of folded paper scattered around. They were John's. He'd left them there. He had this peculiar habit of folding pieces of paper into tiny squares and rectangles, so that when you unfolded them the creases made up these elaborate geometrical designs. Looking back, I suppose it was his way of releasing tension. As far as I know, it's a habit he's held onto through the years. As a matter of fact, one time I went up to Syracuse to visit them and I saw John sitting around folding pieces of paper. "Still with it, huh, John?" I said. "Uh-huh," he said, obviously a little embarrassed that he'd been caught doing what he probably considered a childish thing. "Old habits die hard," he said, and then he stuffed the paper into his pocket. Actually, I felt kind of bad that I'd said anything, because obviously it was something that relaxed him. And me pointing it out probably made him uncomfortable. He wouldn't necessarily show it. Or say anything. But I could tell.

Anyway, John would go up there at night and fold paper and, I guess, daydream. He was always daydreaming. You'd often find him at the dining room table, or just sitting around on the floor, staring into space, like he was in a deep trance. Sometimes, he was in so deep he wouldn't even hear or see you, even when you were right in his face. That's how focused he was. Like he was on drugs or something. I once asked him what he thought about when he dropped into one of those "states." "Oh, just things," he said.

"What kinds of things?"

"I make up stories."

It turned out these stories were nothing more than run-of-the-mill adventure tales boys make up. My kids do it all the time. Only there was a difference with John. All his stories centered around him as a prisoner and his successful attempts to escape. I know because he once told me. For instance, like most boys, John loved war movies. But he especially liked the ones about prisoners of war. He loved The Great Escape. Every time it was on TV, he'd watch it. He fantasized about being held captive in a German prisoner-of-war camp, and he'd make up all these elaborate escape plans, even going so far as to draw maps, where he'd create these tunnels—just like in the movie. Actually, he was quite ingenious at it. Maybe that's because John was quite the one for planning. I remember he once started digging a tunnel under our house, but Dad found out and put a stop to that.

That's why I don't think they'll ever catch him. He's had too much practice disappearing. I'm sure, before he did it, he created an elaborate "tunnel" that would get him out of there. That's just the way John was.

CHAPTER EIGHTEEN:
JANIE McCLELLAN

The first thing I noticed when I opened the door were the flowers he held in his left hand.

"I'm a little late," he said, handing them to me. "I'm sure you've got something to put them in."

I took them from him and said, "I think I can find something. Come on in."

He was wearing a pair of newly washed and pressed, appropriately faded Levi's, black cowboy boots with white piping, a black Levi's cowboy shirt, and a brown tweed sports jacket. His longish, salt-and-pepper hair was slicked back. And as soon as I let him in and he walked past me, I got a good whiff of his cologne. Subtle. Not cheap. This was a man who cared about himself. Maybe a little too much. The kind of guy women like me should avoid at all costs. Sometimes we do. Sometimes we don't. It's a crapshoot.

After taking a second or two to digest this ridiculous picture, I said, "Did you come here to talk about John Hartman or to score?"

He laughed. "Same difference, maybe."

"Hot date later, I suppose," I muttered contemptuously, and then I added, "You're forty-five minutes late."

"Punctuality isn't one of my strong points." He smiled. He wasn't half bad-looking when he smiled. Under other circumstances, I might have found him kind of cute. He was no George Clooney, but he kept himself in pretty good shape physically, which is something I appreciate in a man. And he had an interesting face. I liked his eyes. Blue. Sharp. Focused. Character lines fanning out from the edges. I figured he was in his late forties, the outdoor type, real macho stuff—hunting in the winter, fishing in the summer. Maybe he was a drinker. I didn't think he was married. He wasn't wearing a ring. Not that that means anything. But I just didn't think he was. Maybe because I didn't think his wife would let him out of the house looking like that. Unless, of course, she was from Texas.

"What are these for?" I asked as I headed toward the kitchen to get a vase, with him following close behind.

"To apologize."

"For what? Being late?"

"For the way I behaved today. I was out of line. It was a long day."

"You know," I said, "this is a little screwy. Bringing flowers. And this bullshit get-up you're wearing. What do you think this is, a western hoedown?"

He looked down at himself and grinned, proudly rubbing the lapel of his jacket between his thumb and forefinger. "Not bad, eh?"

I laughed. I don't know why. It wasn't funny. But I couldn't help myself. Nervous laughter, maybe. The whole thing was just so fucking ridiculous. But then I remembered what he was there for and I sobered up. Fast.

I found a vase and filled it with some water.

"Don't forget to put that little packet in. They say it prolongs the life of the flowers."

"You think so?"

"That's what it says."

"Then that's what I'll do." I tore open the packet and poured it in. "There. Happy? Now these flowers will live a long, happy life. Let's go into the living room."

He sat in a chair. I sat on the sofa.

He opened his jacket, leaned back and looked around. "Nice place you've got here." He took out a pen and notebook and a little tape recorder. I sat in a chair facing him. I was about to offer him something, but I caught myself in time. This wasn't a social visit and I wasn't going to be the hostess with the mostest. If he asked, I'd give him something. Otherwise, I just wanted to get this over with.

"Ready?"

I nodded. "To be honest, I'm a little nervous."

"I know," he said, crossing his legs. "I sympathize, but you've got to see my end of it. I have a job to do . . ."

"And you like it, don't you?"

"Most of the time."

"Why's that?"

"Same reason anyone likes their job. Because I'm good at it. Because it's fun. Because it makes me feel important. Because it helps define me as a person. All that crap."

"And it doesn't depress you?"

"Do I look depressed?"

"Not especially."

"Then there's your answer."

"So what about this case?"

"What about it?"

"How do you feel about it?"

He smiled and said, "Yeah, this is a good one. This is one I really wanted."

"Why?"

"Who's supposed to be asking the questions here?"

"You answer mine, I'll answer yours."

He shrugged. "It's not important why I wanted it. It's just important to find out as much about John Hartman as possible. I want to know how he thinks, what his habits are, what he likes to eat for breakfast, what kinds of clothes he likes to wear, what kind of toothpaste and cologne he uses, what his hobbies are. I've got to know how he'd react under any particular set of circumstances. If I can get into his head, then finding him will be that much easier."

"You can never get into anyone's head."

"Don't bet on it."

"You do this for all your cases?"

"Yeah."

"Then you must have an awfully big identity-crisis problem."

"Not a problem. I know exactly who I am." He glared at me. "Now, what say we get started. I'm gonna tape this," he said as he switched on the recorder. It wasn't a question. It was a statement. Small talk was over.

I told him everything, more than I even thought I knew. He was damn good at what he did. One question led to another and before I knew it I was remembering things about John I didn't even know I knew. I was surprised, but it was practically painless. It even started to feel good, in ways I can't explain. I began to feel John take shape inside me, as if I were reconstructing him, one brick at a time, until there he was standing in front of me. It was kind of creepy, actually. But it felt better than having him inside me. Maybe, I thought, now that he's out there, Floyd will take him with me and I'll be free of John forever.

Only once during the almost two hours he spent interviewing me did he break stride and then it was only because my cat, Fritzi, decided to make an unscheduled appearance. She pranced into the room, sniffed at his pants leg, then rubbed up against him, leaving cat hairs all over the bottom of his jeans.

"Shoo!" I said, getting up to chase her away.

"It's okay," he said. "In heat, maybe?"

"I doubt it. She's been neutered."

He winced. "Ouch. Is there no end to man's cruelty?"

"Fritzi, out!" I yelled when she jumped into his lap.

"Don't worry about it. Let her get her kicks."

I shrugged. "Your cleaning bill." Fritzi jumped from his lap and onto the back of the couch where she began pacing back and forth across the ledge behind him. She stopped right behind his head and stayed there, back arched, tail high in the air. It looked like Floyd was wearing this ridiculous furry hat. It was all I could do to keep from laughing. But it didn't faze Floyd. He just kept asking questions, *rat-a-tat-tat,* and writing in his damn notebook. A real pro. Not even a horny cat could unnerve him.

"Would you like some coffee?" I asked when it looked like he was finally winding down. "Or a beer?"

He checked his watch, frowned, and said, "Thanks, but it's late. I'd better be going."

"Wife waiting up for you?" I asked, just to make sure if my guess about him was right.

"If she is, I wouldn't know about it. I'm just one of those poor stiffs paying alimony and child support, waiting for my ex-wife to remarry. There's a nice little reward, not to mention earning my everlasting gratitude, if you know of a likely candidate."

He took a wrinkled card from his jacket pocket and handed it to me. "If there's anything you want to talk to me about, anything you remember, just give me a call."

He got up and now it was time for me to ask the question that was on my mind and probably everyone else's: "Do you think he's still alive?"

"I don't think it, I know it," he said without the slightest hesitation.

"How can you be so sure?"

"Just am," was his answer and, oddly enough, that was good enough for me.

"Do you think he was the one who set his house on fire?"

Floyd shrugged. "I doubt it. He wouldn't be fool enough to come back. The man didn't go to all that trouble to ensure his escape and then risk blowing it by coming back to torch his house. Doesn't make sense." He put his hand on my shoulder and asked, "Are you afraid he'll come back and do something to you?"

"No . . . well . . . maybe a little. But he wouldn't do that, would he? I mean, he'd have no reason . . ."

"No reason at all," he said reassuringly. "You don't have anything to worry about, but if anything does seem out of the ordinary, if you should happen to hear from him, you'll get in touch with me right away, won't you?"

"Yes, I will."

I walked him to the door and then, just before opening it for him, I said, "Did you ever get into something and then, when it was over, want to turn around and say, 'It was all just a big mistake. Let's just erase the whole thing and start over?' "

"All the time."

"So what do you do about it?"

"Nothing. You just try not to make the same mistakes again, because there's no way you can erase what's already happened, Janie," he said, calling me by my first name for the first time. "You'll pull through all right. You've got what it takes."

I don't know why he said that. He didn't know me. He didn't know what I had. Or didn't have. But for some reason it made me feel good. Like I really was capable of getting through it. I opened the door for him and then, just for an instant, I was confused as to why he was there. I almost reached out and kissed him on the cheek. Pretty stupid, huh? Fortunately, I caught myself and instead stuck out my hand. He smiled and shook it.

After he left, I walked back into the living room and noticed

that his hat was still on the coffee table, where Fritzi was circling
it warily, every so often reaching out her nose to sniff at it. I was
going to go after him, but I figured he was long gone, so I didn't.
He'd notice it was missing and come back for it. In the
meantime, I felt good about having that hat there. I felt a little
safer. I don't know why. Maybe it was like some kind of charm
or something. Dumb, huh?

★ ★ ★ ★ ★

PART 3
THE HUNT

★ ★ ★ ★ ★

"For if once a man indulges himself in murder, very soon he comes to think little of robbing; and from robbing he comes next to drinking and Sabbath-breaking, and from that to incivility and procrastination."

—Thomas De Quincey

Chapter Nineteen: John Hartman

I knew they would eventually find them. But I didn't think it would take them as long as it did. I thought a week, maybe two. That would have been a good enough head start. But not a month. That was a bonus. That gave me more than enough time.

I didn't know exactly where I'd wind up. I didn't really care. I just wanted to be far, far away. My plan was to try this and then that and then if they didn't seem right, somewhere else. But since I wanted to change everything, since I wanted to start over, I knew I would start off by heading south, away from where I grew up, away from where I lived the past twenty years of my life. Away from where my life was spinning out of control. I needed to slow things down. I needed to punch the reset button.

Somewhere warm. That's where I wanted to be. A place where my wardrobe would be light and bright instead of dark and somber. One layer, instead of three or four. I would change from black and white to color. And then I would be the real me, the me I could not be.

I'd never been to Florida, so why not there? I could buy a completely new wardrobe. I could find a new job. I could start a new bank account. In the morning, I would leave an empty house. In the evening, I would come home to an empty house. The only sounds that would be made would come from me.

I would become a new me. And that was the point, wasn't it?

And so, Miami it was. At least to start.

At first, it would be like a vacation. I would act as any tourist would. I would do things I would never do at home. Things I could never do at home. That would be the first step. And then, once that was done, I could begin to build a new life by being a new me.

I liked that idea. It suited . . . the new me.

CHAPTER TWENTY:
SOLEIL

One look told me this clown had just flown in non-stop from Weird City, U.S.A. A nutcase if I ever seen one. I should know. I seen plenty in my time. And believe me, there are plenty to see. Me, I go by first impressions and I hardly ever been wrong. My line of work, you gotta be able to spot 'em quick, 'cause your life may depend on it. And I'm not shitting you, neither. This ain't no easy business. It's fraught with danger. You like that phrase? Fraught with danger. I read it in a book one time. I liked the way it sounded. Fraught with danger. I even looked it up to see what it meant. Yes, that's what my life is, fraught with danger. Very fraught.

The eyes. That's the tip-off, sweetie. They always give you away. You can run, honey, but you cannot hide—and I don't care how dark your glasses are. Some have this real wild, weird look in their eyes that can make the hair on the back of your neck stand up and send goose bumps up and down your spine. Some have this kinda creepy, spacey look, like they don't even know what time zone they're in. You know, like that actor. What's his name? Oh, yeah, Chris Walken. I seen him lately on that Live on Saturday Night program. He's scary, honey. Very scary. Like that. Others, they got eyes glazed over heavier than a Krispy Kreme. And some have those beady, close-set, suspicious eyes, and please, honey, don't tell me that don't mean nothing. In his case, the first hint there was something screwy going on was the fact that he'd never look you right in the eye.

And later, when I finally did get a chance to see his eyes up close, in the light, there wasn't much improvement. Blanksville, you know what I mean? Like there was nothin' back there. Nada. Just the wild blue yonder, if you know what I mean. His pupils were all dilated, like he was ripped on coke or something. The Deadeye Dick look, I calls it. This guy had something to hide, no doubt about it. But I'm getting ahead of myself. I do that sometimes. I get ahead of myself.

Anyway, I was working the bar in this sleazy beer joint just off Collins Ave. Things were kinda slow. If you shot a bazooka down A-1A you wouldn'ta hit a fuckin' thing. And no wonder it was Dead City. The weather was for shit and had been for a couple weeks. So the tourists, God bless 'em, were staying away in droves. But then you can never count on the weather holding up in Miami in the winter. And the economy being in the dumper wasn't helping matters, neither. This dude, Obama, maybe he'll get his act together and things'll change. Not fast enough for me. Oh, for another political convention. Two weeks of horny Republicans or Democrats prowling the street for pussy. But no honey, no money, so I was being especially aggressive that night. Not my usual style, which is to hang back and survey the scene, keeping an eye out for someone who looks interested. But in a buyer's market you can't be caught sittin' on your ass keepin' your hands warm. You have to go right out there and get it on. Hustle is the name of the game, sweetie. It's the American way, right? So, that's what I did. Hustle.

He was at the far end of the bar, all by himself, nursing a beer and staring at the bottles lined up against the back wall. He had a couple days' growth of beard and was wearing a pair of baggy tan slacks that looked like they belonged to someone a few sizes larger than he was and a Hawaiian shirt with the tail flapping outside his pants. He looked like a real A-number-1 hick. At first, when I kind of gave him the eye, he looked over, but every time he'd see me looking back at him and smiling, down would go those eyes, right back into his glass of piss-warm beer. He reminded me a little of those fuckin' college kids down on spring break who sometimes come in looking to get laid for the first time, lookin' for someone like me to break their cherry, so's they can brag to their fraternity buddies. They're so nervous they're practically shittin' in their pants and pissin' in their Doc Martens. But they can be kind of cute. But this guy was anything but cute. Even without seeing his eyes I could tell something was up. Experience counts for something, y'know.

Pickings were slim and I could see this guy was at least semi-interested. I knew he'd never make a move on his own, so I decided to take things into my own hot little hands. I moved over, sat down next to him, hiked up my skirt, leaned into him so my boobs pressed lightly against his arm, and said something like, "Hi there, good-looking."

He mumbled, "Hi," without even looking up.

I gave my skirt another hitch up and swung my leg back and forth, making sure the toe of my shoe caught his calf. "You from around here, sailor?"

He shook his head, no.

"Didn't anyone ever warn you against visiting Miami in November, darlin'?"

"Not really."

"Well then, let me be the first. Where ya stayin', if I might ask?"

"Not far from here," he said. Now I knew he was hooked. I touched his arm lightly and said in this sexy little voice I use when I'm working, "Oh, will you look at that. My glass is empty. Mind buying me one? Just for old time's sake."

He looked at my empty glass. "Okay," he said without much

enthusiasm.

"You know, it's kinda noisy here and my place isn't far, maybe we can have that drink there, if you catch my drift."

I don't think he actually said yes, but I do remember him taking out his wallet and paying for the drink he had, leaving a nice tip, too, and then he just up and followed me out the door.

My place wasn't far. He didn't say nothing about having a car and he didn't offer to spring for a cab, so we walked. And then, wouldn't you know it, it started to rain. A sign from heaven, maybe? That is, if you even believe in heaven. Me, I don't think so. You know why? Because if it's like they say, that you see a white light and a tunnel and you get to the end of the tunnel and your mother and father and all your relatives are there to greet you. Well, to me, that ain't heaven, it's hell. I didn't want to see those people when they were alive, so why would I want to spend eternity with them?

Anyway, we got up to my room and I thought I'd probably have to undress him myself, he was so fuckin' passive, but I was wrong. Before I could even get the words "suck or fuck?" out of my mouth, he was all over me, tearing at my clothes, like he hadn't had any in years.

"Hey, slow down, Slick," I said, pushing him away. "I don't like being pawed."

"I'm sorry," he said, and he turned beet red and got this really hurt look on his face.

"It's okay, honey, you just got a little over-excited. It happens. I just like to get things straight before we get started. Now let's find out what it is you want and then, when we get the business end of it out of the way, we can get down to having some fun. You'd like that, wouldn't you?"

He nodded. Didn't say nothing. That's when I got a good look at his eyes. Oh no, I said to myself. I've really nailed one this time. Creep City. Well, what the hell. I figured if things got really hairy I could make it out the door or the window—it ain't like I haven't had to do it before.

He wanted the whole enchilada. No slam-bam-thank-you-ma'am for this boy, but a full night of "ecstasy," and I put that in quotes because I could tell that's just what he expected. Nothing less would do. He wasn't just trying to get off, if you know what I mean. He wanted a fuckin' relationship, for Chrissakes. Well, it was rainin' and business sucked, so what the hell? After all, it wasn't nothing kinky, so I tried for three hundred, got it without so much as a raised eyebrow, and was sorry I hadn't asked for more. Before I could say payment before delivery, he'd whipped six brand new Benjamins and laid them on the dresser. Show time.

And you know, the dude was really somethin' else. I mean, on the outside he seemed all inhibited, but once the lights were out—and he insisted they were—he was, well, what can I say, a real tiger. He kept me up half the night and then he woke me up early and we went at it again. Christ, it was like the poor guy had been marooned on some desert island for the past ten years and I was the first woman he'd been with since the rescue. I never seen nothin' like it. I mean, I had a boyfriend once who never seemed to get enough, but he was nothin' like this guy. At least he came up for air every once in a while. Not this guy. Boom. Boom. Boom. It was almost like he was doin' calisthenics, trying to get in shape. And each time he'd try to outdo what he'd done the last time. And he wasn't half bad, neither. Listen to this: he was actually concerned that I get off, too, which believe me, is damn unusual. Normally, it's ten seconds and outsville, but this guy actually seemed to enjoy foreplay, and I was kinda gettin' off on it, too. Hey, I said kinda . . . it's still a job, you understand.

He wasn't much of a talker. I don't think he said more than two, three sentences the whole time we was together. But then, he wasn't payin' for conversation and that's not what I was there for, neither. Once, though, after the first time we got it on and he was lyin' on his back kind of regroupin', if you know what I mean, I asked him his name. Why? He asked. No reason, I said. You don't want to give me your name, that's fine with me. He said, Paul. I said, okay, Paul it is. Because I knew he made it up. Then I asked if he was married. Just curious. Just making conversation. He didn't answer. I thought maybe he hadn't heard me, so I asked again. He didn't say a word. Instead, he just climbed back in the saddle and screwed me so hard I thought my pussy was going to explode and he was gonna have a fuckin' heart attack. I thought that was a little freaky maybe, but it wasn't as though I didn't have an inkling earlier on. Remember those eyes? Anyway, lots of guys have trouble with their wives and I figured he was another one who just didn't want to talk about it. Okay by me. Talk is cheap, I'm not.

First thing in the morning, sun ain't hardly up yet, he gets dressed, gives me a kiss on the cheek, like I'm his wifey or something and he's rushing off to make the eight-twenty, and he goes to leave.

It was overcast outside, like it was going to pour any minute, and there was this awful chill in the air, so I said, "Hey, will I be seeing you again? Tonight maybe?"

"I don't think so," he said as he opened the door. "I'm leaving town."

"Oh, that's too bad. Hey, have a nice trip, huh? Come back in the spring. The weather's better."

As soon as he closed the door I jumped up to make sure the money was still on the table. Surprise, it was still there. In fact, there was an extra fifty on top of the three hundred. I guess I musta done good, which made me feel okay. Three-fifty for one night's work wasn't bad, especially for the kind of shit-ass season we was havin', so I went back to bed with a smile on my face.

I slept most of the day and when I got up it was still raining. Fuckin' Florida weather.

CHAPTER TWENTY-ONE:
JOHN HARTMAN

I knew they were following me. I knew they would. It was all over the media. Even if I tried to avoid reading about it or hearing about it or seeing it, I couldn't. I tried. I never turned on the TV. Or the radio. Or read a newspaper. But sometimes, when I least expected it, there it was. But the funny thing was, it wasn't me they were talking about. Or writing about. Or showing pictures of. It was someone else. Someone I used to be. Someone I wasn't anymore. Someone I didn't even remember. He was familiar, like someone I might have known somewhere far into the past, or someone I'd read about, or a character in some movie I'd seen. But not me. And so that kind of made it all right.

I wasn't worried about them catching me because I wasn't me anymore. And since I wasn't me, how could they know where I was or where I was going, something even I didn't know? I was sure they thought I had a plan, but I didn't. Oh, sure, there was a plan in the beginning, to get it done, but not anymore. And without a plan, I could do anything, go anywhere, be anyone. And because of that, I had no fear that they would find me. Because I wasn't me anymore. I was someone else. Someone no one knew. Someone I didn't even know. I was a cipher. That's what I was. A cipher. And ciphers aren't people, they are just indications of people. And that's what I was: an indication of a person. And only when I stopped somewhere, in a place where I could take root, would I become a person again.

And then I would be a clean slate. A tabula rasa. I could be anyone I wanted to be. And it would not be the person I was. John Hartman. I could never be that person again. Because that person was dead. Is dead. Along with everything else that was that person.

I am a new person, just waiting to be born.

CHAPTER TWENTY-TWO:
CHARLIE FLOYD

I took the same Kennedy-to-Miami flight John Hartman had, only more than a month later. I even made sure that I got the same seat: 9C, on the aisle, right behind the bulkhead for more leg room.

I wondered how Hartman spent the time between arriving at the airport, parking his car, and his flight south the next evening. A movie? A Broadway show? A good dinner at some expensive French restaurant? Belting back a few at some snazzy night-spot? Or maybe he just checked into the airport motel and spent the night watching TV and jacking off. All the while his family lying there on the cold floor, their bodies losing heat, the breeze blowing through the holes in their heads. But that part of the story wasn't important. At least not to me. Later, maybe, we'd have to piece together all his movements for the record, but now the important thing was to find him.

This is a funny business I'm in. I often wind up reassembling lives, making order out of chaos. I'm an archaeologist, gluing together a stack of old bones, having to know just where one fits with the other, trying to come up with a reasonable facsimile of the way things were. It suits my personality. Loose ends drive me crazy.

If you want to know what I was thinking as I sat in Hartman's seat waiting for the plane to take off, that's what it was. That and the fact that I was following in his footsteps, which was kind of weird. As it turned out, the only difference between

Hartman weeks earlier and me at that moment was that I was traveling under my own name, while he traveled as Evan Portman. It was pretty much the same crew on duty, so when I got the chance I cornered each of them and asked about Hartman. Only one remembered him. She recognized the photo shown to her by one of our junior investigators. She was a sweet blonde with a freckled face and pug nose. Cindy Stephenson, from Evansville, and she remembered him as being your typical traveler. Most of the way down he read. First a newspaper, then various magazines. "He looked normal, like a guy happy to be getting away," she told me.

"He was," I replied.

Later, as we were landing, she sat down in the empty seat across the aisle and said, "That Hartman guy you were asking about, what'd he do?"

"Transgressions against society," I said, "and crimes against nature."

She looked baffled, but didn't press me on it. Instead, she just asked me if I wanted anything before we landed. I said no. Everything was fine the way it was.

The last time I was in Florida was seven years ago. My wife and I drove down one February in an attempt to put the zing back in our marriage. The idea was to get away from the pressures that might be causing the rift. It was a last-ditch attempt to recapture something we probably never had.

It didn't work. Through Delaware, South Carolina and Georgia we fought. I was driving too fast. Who did I think I was, Mario Andretti? I didn't want to stop to eat or use the toilet when she wanted to stop to eat or use the toilet. According to her, I was on a power trip. This was my problem. I had to be in control. "You never know when to let go," she accused. "And you have unreasonable expectations. People are human and by definition we aren't perfect. You can't accept that. You think you're perfect, but you're not."

"That's how well you know me. I'm not perfect and I damn well know. But I'd like to be."

"Yeah. I know. And that's the problem. You actually think you can be and the rest of us suffer because of that."

It probably wasn't the wisest idea, the two of us cooped up in a car for two and a half days. And once we got down to Miami, things didn't get much better. The litany of complaints was endless. The room was lousy. The sun was too strong. The humidity was too high. Too many old people. Too many young people. The traffic was bad. The drivers worse. Was it my fault? Not exactly, but my attitude, she said, didn't help matters. It got so bad that by the time we were ready to check out, I was ready to bash her over the head with one of the sharp-pointed glass ashtrays. I would have pled justifiable homicide.

Eventually, we went our separate ways and I owe it all to Miami Beach.

This is what came back to me as I made my way to the car rental.

From my motel room, The Captain's Paradise, where each room was decorated to look like a ship's cabin, I made a few calls to the local police, to my office to see if anything new had turned up, and then, as an afterthought, to Janie McClellan, but there was no answer. I'm not sure what I would have said to her, so it was probably just as well.

The next morning, I met with Lt. Manny Perez of the Miami PD. Manny's a short, stocky fellow with a pencil-thin mustache and wavy, jet black hair. He's a meticulously dressed Cuban refugee who told me he'd been a professor of American Studies at a Cuban university before he bolted. After the influx of Cuban refugees, he informed me, the Miami PD was looking for qualified Cubans to join the force. The job appealed to Manny because it offered him the kind of security he was looking for.

But there was more than that. His dream was to one day return to the island as part of an invasion force and retake Cuba in the name of democracy. He confided to me that he carried three pistols with him at all times: one in his shoulder holster, one in the small of his back (a trick he learned from watching reruns of the TV detective show Tightrope) and one strapped to his right ankle. Manny suspected Castro had dispatched agents with specific orders to kill those who posed a threat to the Communist regime, and so he was always on his guard.

Manny is a real law-and-order freak and after I gave him the grisly details of the Hartman murders, he was almost as determined as I was to see justice done. "This is a very bad man," he said in a voice that had only a trace of a Spanish accent. His diction was precise and his English vocabulary seemed unlimited, though he occasionally slipped into American colloquialisms like, "We'll burn the sucker's ass" and "Let's get the show on the road," which I think he picked up watching reruns of shows like *Starsky and Hutch*.

"Perhaps he has taken his own wretched life," Manny suggested, brushing lint from his suit jacket as we stood waiting for the elevator at police headquarters. "I don't see how this man could live with himself after what he's done."

"You'd be surprised, Manny. You can't judge criminals the way you'd judge normal human beings. They're different. They've got a fucked-up logic of their own and somehow killing makes sense to them. Either the guy's a complete wacko, in which case a conscience is something he doesn't have, or else he'll have a perfectly legitimate reason for what he did. The reason may sound screwy to you and me, but to him it'll make all the sense in the world."

We made quite a pair, Manny and me. Him, dark-complexioned in his blue and white striped seersucker suit and slim dark tie; and me, pale as a snowfall in Vermont, in my blue jeans, polo shirt and cowboy hat.

First, I wanted to check all the car rental agencies, then try to find where Hartman had holed up in Miami and for how long, which is what we did from his office, which, I think, made Manny very nervous because he preferred to do his work out on the street. We'd been together all morning when I finally said to him as we headed out to get some lunch, "Manny, why not take off the jacket and get comfortable?"

"I am comfortable," he said, stopping to comb his hair in the reflection from a shop window.

"It's fucking 83 degrees, Manny. Live a little. Loosen the tie."

"I'm okay," he said, replacing the comb in his back pocket and smoothing out the sides of his head with his hands. "I don't sweat."

"But I do."

It took us the better part of a day, but we finally came up with something. A man answering Hartman's description had rented a car from a Greyhound office all the way up in Hollywood, the day after his plane landed. He'd used the name Leeland Evans and even had a driver's license to vouch for it. Through the plate number, we were able to locate where he'd stayed: a cheesy motel just off lower Collins Ave., back down in Miami Beach. He'd stayed there three nights.

We worked outward in concentric circles, canvassing the neighborhood to see if anyone remembered him. Day and night we were at it until finally Manny, God bless his Cuban sugarcane cutter's heart, came up with a slightly overweight hooker named Soleil who'd spent the night with him. Needless to say, Manny was damned pleased with himself.

We didn't get much from Soleil, other than the fact that it was Hartman and that he was, in her words, "straight off the boat from Weird City." She kept going on about his eyes giving him away, but she couldn't give us anything concrete, anything that would lead us in his direction. But there was one thing: Hartman or Portman or Evans, he hadn't bothered giving her any name and she hadn't asked, had a three or four days' growth of beard. This meant that he was probably changing his appearance.

When we finished with her, it was back up to Hollywood, where Hartman had returned the car after four days. I figured he must have either settled up there or taken off altogether, so we circulated his photo around the area, hoping to come up with something. In the meantime, I had the bright idea of checking if there were any government records for either Portman or Evans, especially with Social Security. It turned out there was. For Evans. I practically threw my arms around Manny and kissed him because this was a way we might be able to trace him. And we did.

It turned out he'd taken a job working at a garden apartment complex, as a handyman, groundskeeper and janitor. I could feel a jolt of electricity. What if he was still there? Unlikely, but possible. I grabbed Manny and we headed out to the Wiley Street apartments, which consisted of two levels of rental apartments, looking somewhat like a glorified motel. It was late afternoon and the place was empty except for a black man cleaning the pool, which was adjacent to a golf course. We asked him about Evans, but he didn't know anything. Said he'd just started himself the day before. He told us to ask the building manager, who we found in his office watching a soap opera on TV.

"He ain't here no more," said the manager, a middle-aged man with a gut that hung out a good foot over his belt buckle. He was in his late sixties, maybe, with thinning white hair and a sad, hangdog expression on his face. Before he finally got down to talking about the subject at hand, he told us his whole life story and bitched about everything from the government to the unreasonable demands on his elderly tenants, most retirees from the north.

When he finally got down to Hartman, he said, "Soft-spoken, you know, and he seemed like he was kind of intelligent. You didn't have to tell him nothing more than once, not like some of these others. We only paid him $125 a week, but he didn't seem to mind. Sounds low, sure, but a furnished apartment, utilities included, was part of the deal. Not bad, you know. And there's not much trouble here. Mostly retirees from up north— they wade in the pool, they play shuffleboard, they cook their meals, they go to bed early. No noise problems. They're very neat. They live here till they pass on, or until their kids move 'em to assisted living or an old folks' home. He did his work— taking care of the shrubbery, mowing the lawn, seeing to it that the sprinklers worked, taking out the garbage, cleaning the pool, a little painting, stuff like that. No plumbing or electric, though. Unions, that's why. Anyway, he seemed to like workin' with his hands. He never complained about nothing. He seemed happy to have the work. And if there wasn't nothing to do, he found something. Something that needed fixing, maybe. Or he cleaned the pool. He did his work, then at night he'd disappear into his apartment. I think he did a lot of reading, you know. I was in there one time and I saw a lot of books lying around."

"What kind of books?" I asked.

"I don't know. Books. I didn't look at the titles. He read a lot. He wasn't talkative, that's for sure. Very reliable, but not particularly friendly. Kept to himself. He'd say good morning and like that, but not much more. Seemed like he had other things on his mind. Like maybe there was something bothering him."

"He never went out at night?" I asked, carrying the ball alone since Manny seemed like he was keeping half an eye open for Castro's agents.

"Did I say that? Nope. Sometimes, I'd see him take walks. Through the neighborhood, over to the Fed highway and back. Usually late at night, after midnight. I'd hear him come back in around one, two o'clock, if I was still up."

"How long did he work here?"

"Jeez, I guess, well, it was probably only a little over two weeks. He came to me one day and said he had to leave. I asked if there was anything wrong. He said no, he just had to move on. That's not unusual around here. We get a lotta transients. They come and go all the time. Can't keep track of 'em. Sometimes life down here ain't what it's cracked up to be, you know. I would have liked him to stay 'cause he was working out so well, but I knew I'd have no trouble getting somebody else. A job like this ain't hard to fill. You don't need no special skills. No Ph.D. You just have to know how to be polite and do what you're told. I asked him if he needed more money, not that I could have swung it for him, but he said that wasn't it. Could I change his mind? No, he said. So I didn't even try. I gave him his last week's wages and that was the last I saw of him."

"Any visitors while he was here?"

"Not that I saw. Like I said, he kept to himself. He didn't talk to the tenants unless he had to. Didn't even bother having a phone installed. And there was no TV or radio in the apartment, either. We don't put 'em in 'cause they can be stolen too easy."

"How about a car?"

"No. Well, wait a minute, that's not quite the truth. When he first came looking for the job, he drove in. A Chevy, I think. Blue, maybe. But after I hired him, he came back the next day in a cab, with his things."

"What was he carrying?"

"I'm supposed to remember that?"

"Try."

"Okay. Let me think. Maybe it was the one bag. You know, one of those deals that holds a suit and folds over, and kind of a knapsack contraption. Maybe an airline bag, too. But I'm not so sure about that. If he had anything else, I sure can't remember it."

"What brand airline bag?"

"Beats me."

"What did he have when he left?"

"Same as he came in. He called a cab and was gone."

"Did he show any references or anything like that when you hired him?"

"You gotta be kidding. For this kind of job we don't require no references. You just gotta have two arms, two legs, and be breathing. And sometimes two out of three ain't bad."

"Any idea where he went?"

"Nope."

That was it. Nothing, really, other than finding out that he stayed for a while and then, like a bee pollinating a flower, he was gone. Funny, though, that Hartman took a job fixing up other people's apartments when he never bothered to do the same with his own house.

That evening, after thanking Manny and wishing him all kinds of luck with his hoped-for invasion, I hopped a plane back to the cold, sleet and snow.

CHAPTER TWENTY-THREE:
T.J.

Man, lemme tell ya, this jive-ass dude come in just lookin' for trouble and when he got to messin' with me, trouble was what he got. I mean, come on, man, a white dude comin' into a place like this, mouffin' off, bein' disrespectful, what the hell he expect?

It musta been close to midnight and I weren't in the place for more than half an hour. It was the end of the week and my cash was burnin' a real heavy hole in my pants. I was fixin' to have me a real fine time and I got to admit I was flyin' kinda high—a little wine, a little weed—but I was in full control, man, and I wasn't lookin' for no confrontations, if you know what I mean. Listen, I look for trouble, I find it, y'understand? But someone comes on like that, I gots to defend myself and the honor of my friends. He gots no cause ventin' shit like that. No cause at all.

Anyways, I'm at the bar with a couple fine-lookin' young ladies and we're in the middle of some serious shit, if you know what I mean, when this dude comes in, orders a beer, and starts starin' at us, first me, then the young ladies.

"Can I help you with somethin', man?" I say. Not confrontational, y'understand. Just like, y'know, what's your problem, man?

"I don't think so," he says, but real uppity, like I'm beneath him, or something. I mean, this guy has a real attitude, y'understand?

"Well then, whyn't you find someone else to stare at, man.

You're makin' me and my friends here nervous. We don't like bein' nervous, man. We're just here to chill, so whyn't you do the same?"

He looks at one of the women, right straight down at her titties, you'll excuse me, and then this redneck mothafuckah says, "I like what I'm looking at, all right."

I stand up, because I'm not about to let no one disrespect me or anyone I'm with. "Listen, man, whyn't you just take that shit someplace else."

"We ain't botherin' you, baby," says one of the young ladies.

Well, he just gives me this shit-eatin', faggotty-ass smile and says, "Maybe one of you ladies would like to party with me."

"Man," I say, slammin' my beer down on the bar so's it sprays every which way, "you just crossed the god-damned line. Who the hell you think you're talkin' to? Huh? I mean, man, if I was you I'd just get my pale white ass outta here before you get somethin' you don't want. You get my meaning?"

He ignores me and addresses one of the young ladies. "Can I buy you a drink?"

"Man," I say, losin' patience, "I asked you to take a walk. You think you're dealin' with some jive-ass nigger just off the farm? Now get the fuck outta here before they got to carry you out."

"I wasn't speaking to you," he says, pointing his finger at me.

"Hey man, don't you point your fuckin' finger at me, my momma ain't dead yet. Now these ladies is with me, so who the hell you think you are comin' in here messin' with us? You don't belong here, man, so why don't you go back where the fuck you come from?"

"I just thought these ladies were working . . ."

"Working? Shit, man, these are ladies, these ain't no god-damn whores."

"Hard to tell the difference sometimes," he says with this faggotty little smile on his face.

"Okay, man, let's take it outside and settle this, 'cause you just insulted these fine young ladies and I can't have none of that, y'understand?"

"If that's what you want," he says.

So we go outside, out back, in the parking lot, and we have at it. Funny thing is, dude couldn't fight worth shit. He was all mouff. I mean, he hardly put up any kind of fight at all. Man, it was like he wanted to get the shit kicked outta him or somethin'. Shit, I coulda killed the mothahfuckah, and I don't think he woulda give a damn. I mean, he put up his fists and he made like he was throwin' a couple of punches, but he came nowhere close to hittin' me. It was like I was hittin' a damn punching bag. I hit him a couple shots to the gut, then to the face. He went down and then he got right back up and started callin' me a bunch of names, so I hit him again. And again. Finally, he went down and stayed down. And the worst I got for my trouble was some scraped knuckles from beatin' on the dude's face. I guess I got a little carried away, but I was pissed. He had no business actin' like that. No business at all.

When I left him there, he was moanin' and tryin' to get up on his damn feet. At least I didn't kill the mothahfuckah. But I wasn't worried, 'cause I had witnesses who saw him provoke me, and I didn't use no knife or anythin', not that I woulda needed it for that little pussy. But I can't afford no trouble, you know what I mean. 'Cause I got some priors and they'd just love to stick me back in the joint and throw away the key.

That damn mothahfuckah spoiled my damn evenin', man. White mothahfuckah comes into my house and disrespects me and my friends like that, what he expect? Shit, I don't feel the least bit regretful, 'cause he deserved everything he got.

CHAPTER TWENTY-FOUR:
JAMES KIRKLAND

It didn't take long before word was all over town that John Hartman had sent some sort of sinister correspondence to his girlfriend. One story had it that it was a long, rambling, incoherent love letter ending with an ardent appeal for her to meet him at a time and place to be specified later. Another, more ominous story making the rounds was that it was a threatening letter, promising he would return soon and finish her off, too. Still another rumor pegged that letter as a taunting one, a la Jack the Ripper, which she was supposed to pass on to the police. Supposedly, in it he boasted that he would never be found.

The truth, we found out later, was somewhat less dramatic. In fact, it was not a letter at all, but simply a Christmas card, though what was actually written inside was not known by anyone but the police and the woman herself.

And how did I know this? Simple. It's not easy to keep a secret in a small town, especially a secret concerning something like murder.

It's difficult to trace the exact course of the stories, but naturally it started with Janie McClellan herself. From there, in rapid geometric progression, it was disseminated to practically every family in Sedgewick. All this, I might add, as it bypassed the local police altogether.

Not that they didn't learn about the letter eventually. As a matter of fact, in order to quiet certain damaging rumors, especially the one about Hartman threatening to return and do further harm—these rumors were particularly troubling to those who suspected he'd already been back and had set fire to his own house, and my own wife would have to be counted among those—the police finally spoke to reporters and corrected the story. Still, there were those diehards who didn't believe the official account, clinging instead to those other more sinister possibilities.

Of course, talk around town for the next week or two centered around The Letter and John Hartman. Hartman as Madman, to Hartman as Framed Patsy, to Hartman as Heartless Ghoul.

None of these, I suspected, told the story, but I suppose there might have been at least a grain of truth in all of them. In any case, juicy tidbits of information like these were eagerly devoured by every citizen of Sedgewick, and we were all hungry to hear more. We, myself included, treated the whole affair like some kind of TV mini-series and we couldn't wait for the next installment. And when one was slow in coming, when information went from a trickle to nothing at all, someone always seemed to take it upon himself to supply a tasty morsel, whether it was true or not, often one more outrageous than the next. For instance, one absolutely ridiculous story had Hartman as that fellow, D.B. Cooper, who'd hijacked a plane, ransomed a bundle of money, then parachuted out, disappearing into a heavily wooded area in the northwest, only to wind up years later in Sedgewick.

But, after all, these murders were ours. While the people of New York City had Son of Sam, we had John Hartman, and we hugged him to our bosoms. In some odd way, John Hartman became more a part of our community after those murders than he'd ever been while he and his family were living quietly across the street. And we owed him because John Hartman put Sedgewick on the map.

A funny thing happened to me and, to a lesser extent, my

wife and children. Because we lived directly across the street and because I was the one who called the police, it was somehow presumed that we were experts not only on the Hartmans but also on the progress of the case. Friends, co-workers, even people I didn't know would stop me in the street or on my way out of Stop and Shop, or Stop and Slop, as the kids call it, or even go so far as to call to ask me about the case.

At first, I was flattered, and even enjoyed the attention as I became a minor celebrity. I tried to give as honest and detailed answers as I could. But after a while, it became a chore, a burden, an albatross, and I came to resent it. I could understand people's curiosity, I myself had a terminal case, but the invasion of my privacy was beginning to get to me. Besides, in some strange way I felt the situation was mine and mine alone and that I ought to be the one controlling the flow of information. As a result, I began to selfishly hoard any information I had, sharing it only with my wife—usually—and now you. I even got a kick out of withholding as much information as I possibly could from prying ears and, to make matters even worse, I sometimes intimated that I knew much more than I was letting on. But damn it, those murders happened right across the street and I was the one who'd been responsible for the authorities finding the bodies. If it hadn't been for me, who knows how long it would have been before they were discovered. And damn it, I ought to have been the one to tell whatever information whenever I chose and to whomever I chose. It was my story, no one else's, and to suddenly be expected to share part of my life with a rumor-hungry pack of strangers was . . . a crime.

So I became incredibly possessive. Misinformation, even of the most harmless kind, became a personal affront. I wanted to personally set people straight on any ridiculous story that was currently making the rounds. And if there was a book to be written, no offense, I would be the one to write it. That's why I hesitated to speak to you again, when you called. But I realized I was being silly.

My wife, of course, thought I was nuts.

In the meantime, John Hartman began taking over my life. I even went so far as to have imaginary conversations with him on the train to work, or just before I fell asleep. These conversations were full of reproaches as to the nature of his crime, as well as sound, practical advice as to giving himself up. I also tried eliciting the reasons for the murders. Ironically, I spoke to him more in these imaginary conversations than I ever had in life.

But what was worse was that I even began to imagine I'd be the one to find him. Do you know how ridiculous that is? Well, I guess you do. I'm embarrassed to admit I even envisioned myself quitting my job and, like some TV sleuth, running off to bring him back to justice, something no one else seemed to be able to do.

I knew this was off-the-wall and there wasn't, believe me, the remotest chance of my actually doing it. Still, I was at times very close to crossing the line.

And while all this was going on inside my head, I was distancing myself from family and friends, becoming more and more isolated. My own kids began walking around the house twirling an index finger next to their temples in a gesture that meant the old man's off his rocker. I just smiled. What else could I do? I was aware of what was happening to me, but the truth is, I was enjoying myself. Just so long as things didn't get out of hand. But I was aware that things could go too far, that I was alienating myself from the life I'd been living, that I was turning into some kind of oddball myself.

Fortunately, the fantasies stayed fantasies. Nevertheless, they'd better bring him back soon, I thought, or else who knew what I'd wind up doing.

CHAPTER TWENTY-FIVE:
JOHN HARTMAN

Miami did not work out. I did not recognize myself amongst the people who lived there. They were transients. On vacation. Looking for work. On their way to somewhere else. Ready to die. I was not ready to die. I'd already done that. Now, I was ready to live.

When I got beat up, that was the sign for me to move on. I know I brought it on myself and maybe that was planned, like everything else I'd done in my life. Plan. I planned college. I planned work. I planned a family. I planned murder. It was all a plan. Not God's plan. My plan. But plans, no matter how carefully you make them, rarely work the way you think they will. I did not plan for the wife I ended up with. I did not plan for the children I got. I did not plan to live the way I did. On the edge. In debt. Hating what I did. Hating what I'd become. And so, I learned that you have to be nimble. Quick on your feet. You have to be ready to make new plans. Follow those new plans. And then, if they don't work out, make new plans.

I quit that job at the apartment complex, a job I was not unhappy with, but a job that would not get me what I wanted, where I wanted to go. I bought a used car. Not on credit, even though I now had a credit card with my new name on it, but with the cash I brought with me and the cash I earned. Now, I would try going west and see what that brought. West, where the pioneers traveled, where they cleared the land and built houses from scratch, to build a new life. That's what I was. A pioneer. I would push the envelope, moving west, until it was right. Until I found what I was looking for.

And besides, I thought they might be getting closer to finding me. The headlines had faded, but I knew the search hadn't. I knew there were people out there looking for me. I had to laugh because in a way I was looking for me, too. We were all on the same quest.

Who would find me first?

That was the question.

CHAPTER TWENTY-SIX:
MELISSA

Listen, I don't want to give my whole name. At least not my last name. Because if I did, I'd be in big trouble. You know what I mean, right? Everybody probably did the same thing when they were like my age. But my parents, well, they think I'm really wild, out of control. Okay. Like I am a little out of control. But I'm only like twenty, so what's wrong with that? I mean, if you can't be out of control now, when are you going to be out of control? I know eventually I'm going to be married with kids, and then what?

Anyway, so here's the story. I was like on my way back to New Orleans from Fort Lauderdale which, after the big buildup everyone gave it, turned out to be a real snooze. Not much sun, not much surf and the guys were like a bunch of conceited, immature horn dogs just looking to get laid. Talk about your Thanksgiving turkeys. I mean, like my idea of a good time isn't a wet T-shirt contest.

Anyway, it was like time to get back to school. I'd already missed like a week of classes. Well, not really a week, because I have two three-hour classes, so I only missed two classes instead of six. But I had to get back.

My parents would have absolutely killed me if they'd known I'd stayed that long, not to mention how I intended to get back. But like all I had left from my vacation money was like a little less than like twenty bucks and I wasn't about to like blow it all on transportation, since I couldn't possibly ask my dad for any more until at least like the end of the week. As it was, he was like absolutely having multiple heart attacks over the amount of money I'm costing him. He just doesn't understand the cost of living. He's the same way with my mother. He figures she ought to be able to get by with like the same amount he gave her five years ago. No way. Same with me. Besides, women spend more than men, just on the bare necessities. That's another thing he doesn't understand. He looks at how much money my brother costs him and then he compares it to me. What he doesn't understand is that Justin went to school like five years ago and he just doesn't have the same kinds of expenses I do. Like clothing and cosmetics and transportation. After all, he wouldn't want me to hitchhike all over the place, would he? But like that's what I wind up doing. Because I don't have enough money, not because I like it or anything.

I was supposed to like hitch back with my friend, Pam, but she got cold feet at the very last minute and decided to fly. She had almost as little money as I did, but she swallowed her pride (believe me, it was a way little gulp) and called up Daddy, who can't refuse her anything, especially money. So even though he gave her a small lecture on the value of a dollar, he let her charge her ticket on his Amex card.

So with Pam like out of the picture, I was on my own. Sure, I was a little nervous, but what were the chances of anything bad happening. I was going to be extra, extra careful. My plan was to find rides not on the open road, where I couldn't control the situation, but at rest stops and like that, where I could check out people first. Not just like hop into any old car with any old serial killer–type guy.

I had my route all figured out. First, I had to get up to Tampa, then over to Tallahassee and Pensacola, then into Alabama, through Mobile to Baton Rouge, then down into New Orleans. I figured if I was lucky, I'd be able to make it there in no more than a day, depending on the length of my rides.

Unfortunately, things weren't going that swimmingly. Oh, people gave me a lift, okay, but like most of them were only going a few miles. So, like almost six hours after I'd begun, I was like sitting in an IHOP only about a hundred miles from Ford Lauderdale, thinking about maybe calling home for help. But the thought of having to ask my father for money like made me want to puke. He doesn't especially get off on talking to me anyway. Every time I call home he can't wait to put my mother on the phone. Maybe that's like because he's afraid I'm going to like ask him for something, you think?

Anyway, that's when I met this guy who said his name was Donald Sedgewick—he said to call him Don. He was sitting at the table across from me. He seemed like okay, like maybe a little sad, but like okay. I sized him up and decided I could probably hit him up for a ride. He looked like a family man. Now all I had to do was like get up enough nerve to open up a conversation. He had a burger and fries in front of him, which he'd hardly touched. He was just like, daydreaming. I caught his eye and smiled. He smiled back. "Aren't you hungry?" I asked.

He looked down at his food, like he was surprised it was there. "Guess not. Would you like it?"

Weird, huh?

"Oh, no. I just finished eating. Are you like from around here?"

"Just passing through."

"Where to?"

He hesitated, like he wasn't sure. "West."

"That's a coincidence, me too. I go to school in New Orleans. What do you do?"

"Salesman."

"Of what?"

"Of what?" he repeated.

"I mean, like what do you sell?"

"Computers."

"They're like going to take over the world someday, aren't they?"

"Already have."

"Yeah. I guess you're right. Where you from?"

"Connecticut."

"Another coincidence. Like we're practically neighbors. I'm from Scarsdale. I wasn't actually born there, but we've like lived there most of my life. My dad's a lawyer and as soon as he started making like the big bucks, we moved out of the city. I'm a fine arts major. Got any kids?"

"I have."

"How many?"

"Three."

"Any in college?"

"No."

"When it's time, you ought to let them get as far away as possible. It'll be good for them to be on their own. You never know what you can do till you like have to do it."

"I think you're right about that."

"Say, I wonder if like maybe you could give me like a ride, since we're both going in the same general direction and all. To tell the truth, I'm in kind of like a bind. I blew most of my vacation money and I'd rather not spend what little I've got left on transportation. I wouldn't be any bother. Really. I could even like share some of the driving. I'm a real good driver, in case you're worried."

"I don't know how far I'm going."

"Listen, at this point anything would be okay. The last ride I got was for all of seven miles. You'd be doing me a gigantic favor. I'd even chip in something for gas . . ."

He dropped his head. He pushed his fries around the plate. "Well . . . I can't promise how far. I never know when I'm going to stop . . ."

"That's okay. Really."

"Well, maybe as far as Tampa . . ."

"That'd be great. We should be able to make that in like three, four hours, tops. Listen, just let me go to the john and I'll like be right back and we can like get started."

He was a nice man. We talked about all kinds of things. He was like really very well read and he knew an awful lot about art, much more than me and I'm the one who's supposed to be studying it. We got to Sarasota like around three-thirty and it was like really hot so Donald asked me if I'd like to spend like an hour or so on the beach. He said he was getting a cold and thought the sun might do him some good and that he wanted to take a long look at the ocean. I was going to tell him it was the Gulf, but decided like for a change to keep my mouth shut. Then he said we could have some dinner and he'd have me in Tampa right after that. I said okay, why not? In four days I'd hardly seen the sun anyway and I was kind of like enjoying his company. So that's what we did. He didn't bother changing out of his traveling clothes—a polo shirt and chinos—but I changed into a bathing suit and shorts in the HoJo's restroom and we like spent the next hour and a half on the beach. He just stared out into the Gulf. I finally made him take off his shirt and roll up his pants legs. It wasn't much, but it was something.

About four-thirty, we left the beach. Donald decided we ought to head straight for Tampa. We were all grungy from the beach and since he planned to stay there anyway, he'd check into a hotel and we could clean up before dinner. That was okay with me. I was like starving.

I wasn't afraid of him or anything like that. He didn't make a move to hit on me and I could tell he was pretty much harmless. The last thing on his mind, believe me, was getting into my pants.

Anyway, we got there and found this little turn-of-the-century hotel and before we got inside Donald said, "I'm going to book a room for you, too. It'll be late by the time we finish dinner and I don't think you ought to be on the road alone."

"No, please, don't do that."

"I insist. I wouldn't feel right otherwise."

"But the money . . ."

"Don't worry about the money. I'm on an expense account."

"You're going to have a tough time explaining away two rooms."

"I'll use my own money and make up for it someplace else."

"No. If you insist on me staying I'll just bunk down in your room."

I wouldn't let him take no for an answer so we checked into one room, went upstairs, showered, then found someplace to eat. When we got back to the hotel he said he had to make a phone call. Home, he said, to see if everything was okay. He found a phone in the lobby and wasn't gone long.

"No one's home," he said. I noticed he had a hand full of postcards. He asked me if I wanted one to send to my parents. I said like I didn't think so. Remember, they weren't supposed to know I was hitching. I asked him who he'd send them to. He said his kids collected postcards and it was a good way for him to keep in touch. They must have quite a collection, I said. His being a salesman and all.

I knew all along I'd end up in bed with him. 'Cause that's the way I wanted it. He was a nice man and an older man and I'd never been to bed with like an older guy before. At least not older than twenty-eight, twenty-nine. He was shy at first, but like I made it pretty clear I didn't mind it.

He was pretty gentle, actually. He undressed me and then ran his hands up and down my body, his fingers barely touching my skin. I started to get goose bumps. Then he stood up and began taking his clothes off. He was very neat. He took them off and either like folded them neatly or hung what had to be hung. When he finished, he came over, laid down next to me and we started to kiss. It was an incredible turn-on. I'd never had anyone spend so much time on me like that. Just when I thought the whole thing was going to be over, he turned me over on my stomach and started to give me a massage. It was the most fantastic thing . . .

I told him I wanted him inside me. He said, "All right," but the thing was he like wasn't hard yet. He looked like a little embarrassed. I said, "It's okay, I'll take care of it." I went down on him and tried to get him hard, but it just stayed like it was. Finally, I had to give up. I laid back down next to him, put my arms around him and kissed him.

"I'm sorry, Janie," he said.

"Who's Janie? Your wife?"

"No," he said, his face turning red.

"Who, then?"

"I don't know. I just misspoke."

I kissed him again and ran my fingers down his side, like he'd done to me. "Should I try again?"

"No. It doesn't seem to be working tonight. But don't worry, I'll take care of you."

"I'm not worried," I said, but like hardly before I could get the words out he was down like licking my pussy and like not long after that I came.

"You're probably just tired," I said as I ran my hand through his thinning hair. "You've been on the road a long time. Here, just put your head on my chest and go to sleep. We'll try again in the morning. Okay?"

He didn't say anything. He put his head on my chest. His

beard scratched, but I didn't say anything. He seemed to draw into himself and soon it was like he wasn't there anymore. I felt sorry for him, but what could I do? I fell right to sleep. I was tired.

When I got up the next morning he was gone. His stuff was gone. On the dresser, there was a note along with fifty dollars. It said, "Had to leave. Room is paid for and here's some money to get you back to school. Don't hitch. I'm sorry. Goodbye." He didn't sign his name or anything.

I threw on my clothes, grabbed my knapsack and ran downstairs. I asked the desk clerk when Don had checked out. He said about two hours ago. That was close to seven in the morning.

I went outside and there in the parking lot was Don's white Camaro, which was odd. If he'd check out two hours ago how come his car was still in the lot? I figured maybe he was like still around town. I took a walk, looking in stores and restaurants, figuring he might be there. He wasn't. By noon I was back at the hotel and Donald's car was still there. I took a look inside. Nothing. The car was unlocked and the keys were in the ignition. Something very strange was going on. I went back inside and asked the desk clerk if he'd seen Mr. Sedgewick after he'd checked out that morning. He said he hadn't seen him since he got into a cab with his luggage. It was getting late and I didn't feel like hanging around anymore. I went to the bus station and bought a ticket to New Orleans. That's what he wanted, wasn't it?

I guess, considering who he was and all, I was like pretty lucky.

Oh, and I guess I'll like think twice before I like hitch again.

Chapter Twenty-Seven:
John Hartman

I left the car in the parking lot of the hotel because I wanted to zag in case someone thought I was going to zig. I would use public transportation for a while, at least until I got to Arkansas. And then I would buy another cheap car and maybe leave that, too. And I would stop somewhere for a while and get a job. I would make a little money and then move on again. If I did this enough times, I thought, no one would be able to find me.

CHAPTER TWENTY-EIGHT: ENSIGN PETERSON

It was the only seat left on the bus, so I grabbed it. Usually, I like to eyeball the situation, pick me out the best-looking chick, then sit down next to her. But since I was late, I had to settle for what was left. Okay, so those are the breaks. There'd be plenty of time for the other stuff once I hit the Big Easy.

He was reading some kind of serious-looking book. I knew it was serious because it wasn't one of those paperbacks and it didn't have no pictures on the cover. He had a cold. He warned me, but what was I gonna do. He kept sneezing, coughing, blowing his nose, then apologizing. But like I said, what was I gonna do. That woulda been just what the doctor ordered, right? A goddamn cold while I'm on a three-day pass in New Orleans. Shit. But it was my own damn fault for oversleeping.

He didn't talk much. He was either reading his book or studying a bunch of Triple-A maps he kept pulling out of an airline bag. He'd read a while, then all of a sudden, he'd stop and pull out one of those maps and study it like he was gonna take a goddamn test the next day. Every time we'd pass a fucking town, he'd whip out a pencil and mark it off on the map. I was dying to know why the hell he was doing that, but I didn't want to ask him. I was afraid he might talk to me and spray me with a mouthful of his germs.

I kept looking for an empty seat every time we made a stop, but no luck. Wasn't my day, I guess. Bad karma, like they say. Every time we stopped and someone got off, someone else got on and took their place. Well, what the fuck. I was just going to sack out. I needed my rest. I had no intention of doing any sleeping for the next two and a half days. Plenty of time for that later. It was my time to howl. I wouldn't be seeing land for three, maybe four months after that. I needed to get my rocks off.

Sometime near the middle of the afternoon, we stopped long enough to get something to eat. I lost sight of my seat partner for a while because when I got back on the bus he wasn't there. I thought maybe he'd gotten off, but no such luck. Just as the bus was gonna pull out, he gets back on. Evidently, he'd used the time to scout out the nearest drugstore, 'cause he brought half of it back with him. All kinds of things for a cold: Kleenex, nose drops, lozenges, aspirin, cold pills, the works. And the rest of the trip he kept poppin' 'em like they was candy. Finally, I had to say something, 'cause I was afraid he might kick off right next to me.

"Hey, buddy, I don't think that stuff was made to be taken like that. All at once, like. Seems to me I remember something about four hours apart."

He looked at me bleary-eyed, like he couldn't actually focus on me or what I'd said, and then he goes, "It takes more to work on me."

"That so?"

"Uh-huh," he says, wiping sweat from his forehead with his forearm.

"Pill resistant?"

"Guess so. Sorry about this." He shifted his body toward the window, as far away from me as he could get.

"S'okay. We Navy men are tough. Trained to take all kinds of shit, even germ warfare." He looked kinda down, so I said, "Hey, waddya get when you cross a penis with a potato?"

He looked at me kind of strange and said, "I have no idea."

"A dick-tater."

His face broke into a smile.

"Say, you wouldn't happen to be Polish by any chance?"

"No."

"Good, 'cause I got a couple Polish jokes'll knock your socks off. Didja hear about the Polish freedom fighter?"

"No."

"They told him to go out and blow up a truck and he came back with his lips all burnt."

I was a hit. He was laughing, so I told him another. "What do you call a Polack with an I.Q. of 110?"

"Don't know."

"A village."

He laughed so hard, he started to cough. I thought he was going to piss his pants.

"How about the Polish bank. You go in, give 'em a toaster, and they give you five thousand bucks."

Now he was practically choking, he was laughing so hard. "One more. I got one more. Know why they arrested the pregnant Polish woman?"

He shook his head.

"For carrying a ten-pound dope."

So here's the ironic thing for you. I was a regular Bob "Thanks for the Memory" Hope, only I was the troop entertaining the civilian. Gave me a real good feeling. I kinda ran outta jokes, so we just talked a little. Mostly bullshit things. Suddenly, though, he got real heavy and asked if I'd ever killed anyone.

"I'm in the Navy, pal, and there hasn't been much action lately, not since 'Nam, really. And anyways, even if there was, I'd never know if I killed anyone or not. It's all just pushbutton now. Know what I mean? How's about you? Ever in the service?"

"Yes."

"What branch? Wait, don't tell me. Let me guess. Army, right?"

"Yes."

"Yeah, I just had a feeling, you know. Could tell you weren't Navy. You don't have that look about you. Probably an officer, right?"

"Yes."

"Yeah, I knew it. College man, right?"

He nodded.

"Sure. ROTC, right?"

He nodded again.

"Yeah, well, it wasn't tough figuring that one out. I guess that woulda been 'Nam, huh? See any action?"

He hesitated a moment and then said, "Not really." But there was something about the way he said it that I didn't believe.

"So, how's about you?"

"What?"

"Ever kill anybody?"

He didn't answer right away. Finally, he sorta scrunched up his body and whispered, "Yes."

"Really? Man, I guess that's not something you like to think about, huh? I mean, even if it's the enemy."

"They're not always the . . . enemy."

"Well, you gotta figure, they're firing at you, that makes 'em the enemy in my book."

He didn't say anything, just took out a Kleenex and started wiping his eyes.

"Look, let's change the subject, okay? But remember, you was the one who brought it up."

"Yes. I know."

"So why was that?"

"It just came to mind."

"Look, they train us to kill and sometimes that's just what

you got to do, that's all. It's a job, like anything else. That's the way you got to look at it. Sometimes it's the right thing to do, you know. I'm not condoning killing or anything like that, but sometimes it's gotta be done. Someone attacks you or your family or your country, well, you gotta do what you gotta do. Anyway, it was a long time ago, right? You can't let it get to you now. It's past history. You shouldn't feel guilty about it. What's done is done, and you can't take nothing back."

After this, he kinda crawled back into his shell. He stared out the window for a while, then went back to doing his map thing. Okay by me. I didn't want to talk about a downer like that, not with two and a half days of New Orleans in front of me.

When we pulled into the bus station he asked where I was going to stay. I told him the first place that struck my fancy and didn't cost an arm and a leg. I asked him where he was staying. He said he didn't know. It was his first time in New Orleans. He said he was just passing through on his way to Texas. I don't know why, but I asked him if he wanted to have a drink with me. He was probably the last guy in the world I wanted to spend time with, but I guess I kinda felt sorry for him. I don't know why. He thought about it a minute, then said okay. I told him I'd meet him at a particular bar on Basin Street around eight-thirty. He said okay. I waited for him, but he never showed. Okay, I didn't wait all that long, but I wasn't about to waste too much time waiting to have a drink with some guy I hardly knew, some guy I didn't even like that much.

I didn't think I'd ever see him again and ask me if I cared, but the next night, as I was walking down the street with some girl I picked up at a club the night before, sure enough, I bump into him. Hey, they say it's a small world, right? He was wearing the same clothes he'd worn the day before, and probably the day before that, too. He looked a little messed up. How? Well, like skuzzy, you know. Like he hadn't showered or nothing.

"Hey, how ya doin'?" I said. "Missed you last night. Musta got our signals crossed." I didn't want him to think I blew him off.

He seemed sorta in a daze. "Yeah. Sorry. I got hung up."

"S'okay by me, pal. I had plenty to keep me occupied. This here's Sonya. Sonya, this here's . . . sorry, pal, forgot your name."

"Elliot."

"Yeah, this is Elliot. Met him on the bus into town yesterday. Wanna join us for a drink, man?"

"I don't think so."

"Aw, come on, just one. We'll go right in there. Lemme buy you one. Anyone who laughs at my jokes deserves a drink. Okay?"

So I bought him a drink. How does he repay me? By fuckin' comin' on to my girl, that's how. I fuckin' couldn't believe it. There he was, right in front of my fuckin' face, saying all kinds of things and touching her all over. Jesus, what kind of shit is that? Here I was just trying to be friendly and he's putting the moves on my woman, and he ain't even subtle about it. What kind of lowlife was this?

I was sorely tempted to let one fly, but I held back. Why? Because I thought there had to be something seriously mental with this guy, that's why. I mean, listen, here I was trying to be nice to him and he ups and turns on me. This is some kind of psycho, right? So I decided I just oughtta get the hell out of there before I did something I'd regret.

"Come on," I say to Sonya, grabbing her arm. "We gotta get movin'."

"What's the hurry?" he says.

"Yeah, what's the hurry?" she repeats, which burned my ass. It was all I could do to keep from dumpin' what was left of my drink on her. But that woulda been wasteful, right?

154

"The hurry is 'cause I say it's time to go, that's the damn hurry. And furthermore, pal, if you wanna know what the damn hurry is, it's because I don't like the way you're behavin' here." I stood nose to nose with him. "You gotta problem with me?"

"No problem," he says, looking away from me.

"Don't look away from me, pal. I'm talkin' to you. You got a problem, you share it with me. I wanna know what the hell's wrong with you. Hittin' on this lady right in front of me."

"Nothing," he says.

"Okay, so it's nothing. We'll just leave it at that. Now, we're gettin' the hell out of here." I look at Sonya. "That okay with you?"

She nodded.

"And you?"

He don't say nothing.

So we left. To this day, I don't know what kind of bug got up his ass, but if you ask me, he was a real loony. You know, sometimes you run into people like that. They got what you call a death wish.

It ain't a pleasant situation. Sometimes it kinda makes you wanna just keep to yourself, not get involved with anybody, don't it?

Now, of course, the cops have talked to me and I'm talking to you, so I kinda understand what was going on there. But back then, I just thought he was another run-of-the-mill creep.

CHAPTER TWENTY-NINE:
CHARLIE FLOYD

I'm not one for psychological bullshit, but occasionally there's something to it. I mean, look at it this way: I've seen smart guys, and I mean really smart, get tripped up by something so elemental you'd think you were dealing with an absolute moron with nothing but wind blowing through their ears. They do stupid, careless things like dropping an incriminating book of matches, leaving fingerprints, never changing their m.o.'s to throw us off, something that leads us right to their door. It's the need to be caught, or at least the need to be noticed.

It's the dark, flip side of the celebrity thing. Now I'm not saying Hartman killed his family to be noticed, but I am saying once he did what he did, he wasn't about to sing, "Thanks for the memory," and tap dance off the stage.

That's the way I saw this Hartman Christmas card thing. Just a way for him to stay center stage a little while longer. He had to let us know he was still out there, that we shouldn't stop looking for him, as if I would. And maybe this was just the thing that would lead us to him.

I got back to Sedgewick late Friday afternoon and went straight to the Chief's office to take a look at the card. It arrived in a plain, white envelope, postmarked Mexico City, with no return address. It had been mailed a week and a half earlier. It was one of your run-of-the-mill sappy Christmas numbers with a tree and tiny angels dressed in white dancing around it, next to a fireplace hung with care. Printed inside, under the card company's wishes, in a barely legible scrawl, was Man proposes and God disposes. Ho! Ho! Ha! Janie, darling. I'm sorry. Please forgive me for everything and have a wonderful Christmas. Love, J.

The card was soiled and bent out of shape, like it'd been carried around in a coat pocket for some time before finally being mailed. By the time I saw it, it had been dusted for prints and the handwriting checked. The prints and writing were his. At least that would silence the jerks who thought Hartman was among the dearly departed.

I called Janie McClellan at her office, but she wasn't there. So I went to her house.

She was understandably distraught. Here she was doing her damnedest to forget Hartman and he sends her a fucking Christmas card. Reality and him had a very nodding acquaintance, at best. Not satisfied that he'd killed five, he's got to add another victim to the list. Only this time, he's fucking with a mind: psychological murder. I was pissed.

"I'm glad to see you," she said hoarsely. She was wearing loose-fitting jeans—she looked like she'd lost weight since I'd last interviewed her—and a bulky, white cable-knit sweater. Her hair was tied back in a ponytail and she wore no makeup. She looked like she hadn't been getting much sleep.

"How are you doing?"

"Not so hot," she said, leading me into the living room.

"Yeah, so I see. Tell me about it."

"What's to tell? I came home from work, grabbed my mail, and there it was. I can't believe it . . ." She started to cry, but stopped herself. "What does that creep want from me?"

"Nothing. It has nothing to do with you."

"I want out of this," she said, her voice cracking. "I want it to fucking stop. I want him to stop."

She started to cry again. I didn't know what to do. I never

do, when women cry. Suddenly, I'm aware of every part of my body. My arms go limp. My legs want to move. Away. But they don't. Because I'm frozen, physically and emotionally. I'm aware of the expression on my face, which seems to be nothing less than dumb.

"It'll be over soon," I said. "We're going to get him. Believe me."

"It won't end then . . ."

"Yes . . ."

"Don't bullshit me. You know as well as I do the only thing that'll end this for me is if he's dead . . . and even then . . ."

I didn't know what to say, so I steered her back to the card. "Tell me about that 'Man proposes, God disposes' business."

She shrugged and pulled away, moving toward the kitchen. "How should I know? Do you want something to drink?"

"A beer maybe?"

"Sorry. . . ."

"Nothing, then. Got any ideas?"

"He was always quoting poetry. It's probably just another goddamn poem. What was it, 'God proposes and man disposes'?"

"Other way around."

"Well, it's got God in it, so why not ask the good Reverend? John always had something to say about him," she added sarcastically.

"What's that supposed to mean?"

"Nothing. He just thought he was a hypocrite, that's all . . . and incompetent to boot."

"Incompetent how?"

"Because he couldn't convince John of the existence of God. John used to make fun of him. He'd say the Reverend might as well have been a shoe salesman for all the good he was doing.

He said, 'What the hell good is he, if he can't teach me to have faith?' "

"So he wanted to learn faith, did he?"

"Doesn't everybody?"

"Some of us already have it, babe."

"Oh, yeah. Like in what?"

"Myself."

"You think that's enough?" she said, folding her arms across her chest so that her breasts were pushed up slightly.

"For now it is. When it's not, I'll find something else. In the meantime, maybe I ought to have another talk with the Rev. You know, it ain't easy selling God. I mean, with shoes at least you've got them right there in front of you. You get the customer to try them on, walk around the store, take a look in the mirror. If he doesn't like what he sees, there's no sale and you just show him another pair. It's a lot easier than selling God."

"Well, if you think the Reverend's going to help you find John, give it a shot."

"Uh, there's something else I need to ask you. A couple of things, in fact."

"What are they?"

"First, did you ever meet his wife? I'm trying to get a bead on her, but it's tough. She didn't seem to have any friends. Kept to herself."

"You think maybe we spoke on the phone regularly?"

"I thought maybe you bumped into her."

"Well, as a matter of fact, I did. Once. I didn't speak to her. It was in the supermarket. She was on the checkout line in front of me. I recognized her from a photo John had of her and the kids on his desk. She was kind of spooky. She had this see-through skin. It was so white and thin you could actually see her veins. I remember thinking it was kind of ironic because from what John told me about her she seemed like such a tough customer, and here her skin was so thin you could almost see through it. I just saw her that once and I didn't like her. But it wasn't because of what John said about her. It was just this strange aura she had about her. I can't explain it."

"Nothing else?"

"No."

"I wish I could offer you some kind of protection, but I can't."

"Protection from what?"

"From Hartman."

She shook her head slightly and it seemed that the beginnings of a smile formed on her lips. "I don't think I have to worry about that. He's not coming back. To what? To what would he come back? No, he's just fucking with us. That's what he's doing."

The next morning, early, I made a special Saturday visit to the office. I hadn't bothered unpacking my bag and I was ready to wing it down to Mexico City, but the boss tried throwing a monkey wrench in my plans.

"We can't afford it," he said.

"What do you mean? The fucking state of Connecticut can't afford to send me down to Mexico for a couple days? The whole fucking state can't scrape together enough dough for that?"

He threw up his hands. "How do I reconcile it? We've got priorities, Charles."

"Fuck priorities. As far as I'm concerned, this is a priority."

"The FBI is on this. So's Interpol. Let them do the legwork. They've got the resources, we haven't."

"Shit, Ed, they've got hundreds of other cases to take care of when they're not busy chasing down terrorists. You think they're going to bust their humps on this one? This is the only one I've got. Besides, you owe me. I've worked a lot of shit-ass cases for you over the years and I never opened my mouth. Not once. I don't ask for favors."

"But you're asking for this one."

I just looked at him. "Okay, you're right," he said. "I do owe you. Besides, I don't have the heart to fight you on this one. So I'm gonna throw out the book and let you go. But listen, Charles, there's a bottom line here. I'm not gonna let you chase all the hell over the world looking for this guy. When it becomes a matter of diminishing returns, then you're off it. Understand? And I'm the one who decides when to pull the plug, not you."

"Understood. And don't think I don't appreciate it, Ed. You're a helluva guy."

"Cut the crap. Kissing ass doesn't become you. I know you too well to buy any of it anyway. But I want a strict accounting, and keep those expenses down, understand? The last thing I need is some blue-nose, bureaucratic political asshole running up my ass about the budget. When it comes down to lives versus money, you know which way they're gonna come down. And do me a favor, huh? Check in. I want reports. And remember, this is a foreign country you're going to and things can get dicey. I don't want you going down there and getting lost. And I don't want any international incidents, either. The Connecticut National Guard ain't gonna march into Mexico to save your sorry ass. You hear what I'm saying, Charles?"

"I hear."

I made arrangements for a noon flight to Mexico City the next day. When I got home, I ordered a pizza and turned in. My body was tired, but not my mind, so I couldn't fall asleep. I got up and found the photograph of John Hartman. I studied it. I started thinking how I was going to track him down. I thought that might help put me to sleep, but it didn't. My mind kept wandering. I thought about Janie McClellan. I thought about starting another life. I thought about going to Mexico and never coming back . . .

The telephone rang. It was Claudia, my ex-wife. She wanted to know where the check was. "For Chrissakes," I said, "it was just due last week. Give me a break. I was away."

"Don't give me any stories, Charles."

"It's not a story. I was working. I forgot. It'll be in the mail tomorrow. Anything else?"

"Just that."

"How are the kids?"

"Fine."

"Next weekend, okay? If I'm back."

"It should be okay. Call first."

"I will. Anything else new?"

"No."

"Then have a nice weekend," I said and hung up. The bitch. I gave up the idea of sleep and turned on the TV. Sometime later that night, not much before dawn, I finally fell off.

CHAPTER THIRTY:
JOHN HARTMAN

I'm tired. I'm always tired. And yet it's hard to sleep. Very hard. The only time I can sleep is when I'm moving. On a bus. Or a train. Or a plane. Or a car. Maybe it's because it seems like I am going somewhere. Not standing still. I am moving. Moving. Moving. Ahead. Away. Far away. From here. From everywhere. And when I'm not moving, I'm going nowhere. Not ahead. Not behind. When I'm not moving, I am in one place. Sedentary. Motionless. Frozen in time. Like the bodies lost on Everest. An arm or a leg sticking out of the frozen snow. Climbers pass them by, but don't even notice them. They are part of the landscape. They are not there. But they are. Like me. And so I need to move. And so I am moving. Always moving.

But sometimes it feels like I am moving backward. I am behind me. Somewhere I don't want to be. And so I cannot look back. Only forward. In back of me there is nothing. In front of me, there is something. Anything. Behind me, there is nothing. I am nothing. In front of me, maybe I will be something. Something else. Something I want to be. I don't know what that is, but if I keep moving I will find out. If I stop, I will only be me. And so I keep moving. Forward. Ahead. To somewhere else.

I don't know where I'm going. But I'm going. I am excited about where I'm going, even though I don't know where that is. But I will be someone else there. I will meet new people. I will make a new life. I will be not who I am but someone else.

Someone I was not. Someone I do not hate. Someone who does not hate me.

I will start over. And over. And over. And I will never look back. Never.

Chapter Thirty-One:
Ralph Newsom

Nice guy. Kinda quiet. No trouble. No trouble at all. Came in one afternoon, asked if I had any work for him. Just so happened the kid who worked nights up and quit. We're 24/7 and I ain't got the kinda energy to work more than five eight-hour shifts a week, so I had to replace him.

"Good timing," I said.

"You mean you have something?" he said.

"Just so happens I have. But it's the night shift. Kinda quiet then." I looked at him closely. I got a thing about people. I can size them up pretty quick. I can't exactly say what it is, but I kinda got a gift, if you know what I mean. I can tell if someone's reliable or if they're a fuck-up. This guy, he was reliable. He was neatly dressed. Trousers, not jeans. Button-down shirt, tucked in, not waving to the wind, like the kids wear 'em today. His hair was cut. Not down to his shoulders, not that I got anything against long hair, you understand. He just looked like he could be relied upon. Not that you got to be a genius to do this job. You stand behind the cash register and you take money. You fill the shelves when new stock comes in. You price the stock. You mop up the floors. You spot trouble, you call 911.

"I'll take it."

"Ain't you even gonna ask how much it pays?"

"Oh, yes. How much?"

"Seven bucks an hour. You still interested?"

"Yes."

"I gotta tell you, it's kinda boring. Nothing much happens here between eleven and seven."

"That's okay. I like to read."

"Well, that's good."

"When can I start?"

"You come back tonight, around ten o'clock, and I'll teach you what you got to know."

"Okay," he said, and stuck out his hand, to seal the deal. He was a real gentleman. He worked here for a month, maybe more. Not one complaint about him. He did his job and he did it well. And when he left, he didn't just up and disappear. He gave me a week's notice. Said he had a family emergency, back east, I think. He asked me if I knew anyone who might want to sell him a car, cheap. Just so happened I had one sitting in my driveway. It worked fine. Just didn't use it anymore. So I sold it to him. Cheap.

CHAPTER THIRTY-TWO:
JOHN HARTMAN

Once I left Louisiana and hit Texas, crossing the border from Shreveport into Longview, I drove southwest, through Waco, Killeen, and Roundrock, until I hit Austin, my destination. I'd heard a lot about the city. It was a mixed bag. Whites, Blacks, Hispanics, Asians. It was more tech oriented than I thought it would be, and it was filled with students. I'd had enough of students. Of young people. They cannot be controlled. They are unpredictable. It was then I realized that in order to be born again, I had to find a different womb. I had to leave the country. Keep moving south, into Latin America. It was there I would be safe.

And so I drove. I drove through San Antonio, to Nuevo Laredo, where I would cross the border into Mexico. I stopped only to eat and relieve myself. And when I was too tired to drive, I pulled into a cheap motel, where I stayed the night. The next morning, I was on the road again. I drove fast, as fast as I could. Within the speed limit, of course. I could not afford to be stopped. I had to stay within the law. I was a law-abiding citizen now. My only transgression was behind me. Way behind me. In another life. Committed by another man.

I would go through Monterrey, heading toward Mexico City, where I could lose myself. And then, I would emerge a new self. And I would start over. And things would be better. The ghosts would be gone.

Chapter Thirty-Three:
Jerry, the Barfly

I'm sitting at the bar, quaffing a few beers, trying to watch the hoops game on a TV set with the color all shot to hell. Faces were red and the hardwood was puke green. But I didn't give a shit. The game was on. I was with my buds. And the beer was flowin'. Now who was playing? Let me think. I oughtta know. If memory serves, I had a few bucks on the game, just to make it interesting. I know it was a college game. I think maybe it was one of the Big Ten teams. Michigan, maybe. Or was it Ohio State? One of those. What the hell difference does it make? They all play and look pretty much the same. Big, brawny guys, most of 'em black, who look like they play football in the off-season. Football. That's my game. That's everyone's game in Texas. Hook 'em horns! The Cowboys. But it was a Friday night. Hoops night. Wait a second. Now that I think of it, I do remember the other team. Duke. Yeah. Duke. Sure enough, I remember Coach K almost getting a tech called on him. Helluva a coach, that one. Son of a gun hardly ever loses. Boom. Boom. Boom. Keeps turning out winners. That's what I call a coach.

Anyway, I'm watching this game at the bar because I couldn't watch it at home. My wife, she's the reason. She gets on my case. Always on my case. I'm drinking too much beer. It's not good for me. I'm smoking too much. It's not good for me. I'm eating too much. It's not good for me. I don't get enough exercise. It's not good for me. I'm watching the fucking basketball game and she's telling me all these things that ain't good for me. The bottom line is, I'm watching the game on the tube and that's not good for her. She don't want me to watch the game on the tube. She wants to watch a movie. Or Oprah. Or Dr. Phil. Or Judge Judy. Or one of them reality shows. She likes the dancing one. And the singing one. And the one where those jerks get kicked off the island. Or God knows what. Shit. Pure shit for the masses. I'll take a hoops game any old time. That's reality.

So I go out. That's why I was in that joint when this guy sits down next to me. He's a hoops fan, too. I can see that right away, just from the way he's watching the game. He knows what he's looking at. All the nuances. The ebb and flow of the Big Mo. He sees the beauty in the game. He sees the grace. He sees the human fucking drama. First you're up, then you're down, then you're up again. But if you don't watch out, if you don't keep your eyes open and your mind on the fuckin' game, you'll find yourself going right down the tubes. The game is always changing, you see. It's alive. Even the one-sided games have the possibility, up to the very end, of surprising you. All sports are like that. That's what I love about 'em. Sometimes the underdog wins, and there's nothing more inspiring than seeing a loser turn things around and become a winner. You know what I mean? It's all about focus. That's the name of the game. That's what sports are. I don't care how much talent you got, if you don't focus, wiping everything else out of your mind except the game, then you're a loser. And it takes a real sports fan to know that. And this guy, he was a real sports fan. He knew his hoops. He knew about focus.

Me, I like the pros best. I know there's something to the amateurs, namely playing the sport for the sheer beauty of the game, not the money. But no one does that anymore, anyway. They're all in it for what it can do for them. So why not watch the best, right?

But the guy next to me don't think that way. He likes the college game. "Why?" I ask.

"I don't like the perfection of the pros," he goes. "Imperfections are more interesting," he goes. "The college game is more interesting because there's more of a chance for failure, for mistakes. There's more strategy, too. It's not just run and gun."

"I've got to agree with you there, but what's wrong with perfection?"

"It's . . . dull," he goes. "And predictable. And . . . impossible."

"I don't get you. First you tell me you don't like the game because it's perfection, then you tell me perfection's impossible. Which is it, pal? Make up your mind."

He takes a swig of his beer, wipes his brow, 'cause it was hot in there, and goes, "There's perfection in the short run, maybe, but in the long run, never. A little bit of failure is okay. It's just that when it gets to be too much . . . well, it destroys . . . initiative . . . it destroys . . ."

"You mean like a team on a fifteen-game losing streak?"

"I suppose."

"Well, I guess that's what makes horse racing, don't it? You like college, I like the pros. We agree to disagree."

"Yes," he goes, finishing up his beer.

"Here, let me buy you another one," I go.

"Thanks," he goes.

I get him another. We're startin' to, you know, what they call bond. That's why I like hanging out in bars. You get a chance to get close to another guy for a coupla hours and then maybe you're never gonna see him again. But for those coupla hours, you're close, and that's important, know what I mean? This guy had something on the ball. He wasn't all that easy to get close to, but he was warmin' up, and that was okay. I give him my name and ask his. Joe something or other, he says. I don't know whether I wasn't listening good or whether he was mumbling. Anyway, Joe's the only part I got. But two guys talkin' in a bar, what's the difference? First names are all you need, right? You ain't gonna marry the guy, right? You're just shootin' the breeze over a couple of brews.

"Where you from?" I go.

"Up north."

"Yeah? That so? Me, too. Came down here a coupla years ago 'cause of the job situation up there. It stunk. I work construction and there was nothin', and I mean nothin', going on up there, so I came down here. Lotsa work down here. Condos going up all over the place. It's tech, man. Money flows in because of them little chips and such. I don't get rich, but I make an okay living. And the weather, well, even though it stinks lately, it sure as hell beats Illinois. Now I'm a Texan, man. Look here, I got the boots to prove it. Where exactly you from?"

"Lots of places," he goes.

"Ever lived in Chicago?"

"No."

"What do you do for a living?"

"Right now?" he goes.

"Now. Before. Later. Whatever."

"Computers. Banking. But that was before. Now, I'm just traveling."

"Family?"

He shrugs and says nothing for a second or two. I jump in before he can answer. "Am I being too nosy? I mean, I'm just trying to make conversation here. If I'm out of line, just tell me. You won't hurt my feelings. Hell, my wife says I ain't got any."

"No," he goes. "It's okay . . . I don't have a family anymore."

"Divorced, huh."

"No."

"Well, I think I'll stop there. I can see it's a sore spot."

He takes a drink, stares at the TV, where nothing in particular is happening, and then he goes, "They were killed . . . in an accident."

"Jeez, that's tough luck. I'm real sorry about that, pal. Christ, it's a wonder you're still walking around in one piece. Car?"

He don't answer. He orders another drink. He orders me one, too. The second half is about to start and the first-half statistics are up on the screen. I want to take a look, just to see how my guys are doin' field goal percentage wise, but I don't want to be rude.

"So, I guess that explains all the travel, huh? How long you been on the road?"

"A couple of months," he goes. I feel a definite chill in the air. But I feel sorry for the guy. It looks like he's had a rough time lately.

"A coupla months, huh? Hey, listen, if you want a good home-cooked meal, why don'tcha come home with me? My wife bugs the shit outta me, but she can cook. I'll give her a call. How's about it? Tonight. She won't mind. It'll give her someone else to talk to. She's always complaining I don't say nothing at the dinner table. How's about it?"

"No thanks," he goes. "I'm leaving tomorrow. I've got things to do."

"Yeah, well, I understand. Where to?"

"Mexico, maybe. I've always wanted to see Mexico."

"Not much down there but wetbacks trying to come up here, but suit yourself."

"I will," he says.

CHAPTER THIRTY-FOUR:
CHARLIE FLOYD

A guy I once knew swore he saw God while sitting in a dentist's chair.

I didn't consider him crazy, despite this bizarre admission, which, let's face it, was probably nitrous oxide–induced. Between you and me, I figure that's about as close as I'll ever get to meeting God personally. This is okay by me because, to tell the truth, religion and me aren't exactly on the best of terms. I was born a Catholic, but I haven't seen the inside of a church since, well, since my wedding, and then only because my wife insisted. I'm not anti-God, it's just that religion has a way of complicating things. It puts up barriers between man and God. The way I see it, the battle is strictly one between Good and Evil, and since basically I usually find myself on the side of Good, I figure I don't have too much to worry about.

Religious people give me the creeps, especially the ones who wear it on their sleeves—or collars. I can't help feeling there's something else going on behind the scenes. That maybe they've got some kind of angle they're working, or a hang-up. I suppose this tells you more about me than it does about them, but that's the way I feel. I might be able to change, but it would take a little more than a visitation by God while sitting in a dentist's chair.

So you can imagine how I felt meeting the Reverend again. But it was part of my job—leave no stone unturned, no witness unexamined—so that's why I did it. What I do. And, after meeting with him the second time, I had to admit Hartman wasn't too far off base about the guy. He was a zero in my book. A big, fat zero. I knew he meant well and I suppose that counts for something, but I've seen guys guilty as sin of murder and worse who were less circumspect about what they said than he was. I mean, this guy couldn't commit himself at Friendly's to vanilla or chocolate. Maybe. Could be. Perhaps. Might. These were the words that took up an awful lot of empty space in his answers. And when I gave him the "Man proposes, God disposes" lines Hartman had penned to Janie, he was completely stumped. He started to tell me what they meant. Literally.

"I know what they mean, Reverend," I interrupted. "I'm just trying to find out what they might mean to Hartman."

He hemmed and hawed, but the bottom line was he hadn't the foggiest idea. He supposed the lines were meant ironically, since Hartman was one of, as he put it, the "wavering flock." That didn't do me a hell of a lot of good, especially since that description fits a good two-thirds of the population of this country, me included.

Back to the wavering flock, Reverend. For me, it was on to Mexico City where, I had this feeling in my gut, I'd find Hartman.

During the flight, I reviewed what we had:

As far as we could tell, Hartman began to put his plan into motion about the time he was fired from his job—early October. Evidently, his family knew nothing of his being out of work, since Janie covered for him. So, we could assume that for the next two weeks at least, he left home every morning at the same time and returned by six, six-thirty that evening. This left him free pretty much the whole day to plan and prepare for the murders. The weapons were no problem. He had two pistols he'd picked up in the service and we found he'd gone at least twice to a pistol range in Hartford to test-fire them. Approximately one week before the murders he had a phony prescription for Ambien filled at the local pharmacy, which we verified not only with the druggist but with the Reverend, who happened to bump into Hartman as he was leaving the store.

After he had the weapons and the sleeping pills, he made a trip down to New York and made four separate airline reservations at four airlines under four different names. Each was for a different destination and different time of day. That same afternoon, the postal authorities in Sedgewick have a record of receiving a call from Hartman asking them to halt mail delivery as of Monday, November 3, until further notice. On Friday, Hartman made a call to his sister in West Virginia, telling her he was taking the whole family, mom included, on a two-week, maybe longer, holiday in the Caribbean. She wished she could go, too. Maybe next year, Hartman said. This was to be just for his immediate family. A bonding experience, he explained.

On the day of the murders, Hartman phoned the Reverend and told him he and his family would be away for an extended period of time and that his son, Paul, would not be attending Sunday school for at least a few weeks and that his mother wouldn't be attending Sunday services for the same period. He also canceled newspaper delivery indefinitely.

We lost sight of Hartman for the rest of the day, but at four o'clock in the afternoon he phoned the principal of Sedgewick High and informed him of a planned family trip to Chicago, a trip that would keep the kids out of school at least until after the Thanksgiving holidays.

By six o'clock Hartman was back in his house. Maybe he spent the evening watching TV with his kids, or upstairs in his den, reading. We found a book of poems and essays by Alexander Pope on his desk. The page was open with this passage underlined:

"As Man, perhaps, the moment of his breath,

Receives the lurking principle of death."

As close as we can figure, around ten o'clock or so, the murders began. He gave his wife and mother tea with the sleeping tablets, his kids hot chocolate cocktails with the same added ingredient, the remains of which were found in the victims' bodies. Within an hour or so, according to the medical examiner, they were in lullaby land. Once asleep, he carried each one of them into the main ballroom on the first floor and placed them on blankets he'd neatly folded in half. Then he shot them. In the head. It was probably some time after that he went back upstairs where he shot his mother as she slept in her bed, and then he took care of the family dog. All this he accomplished with his .32 caliber revolver, which he then cleaned and oiled and put in a dresser drawer.

Now it was clean-up time. He went downstairs and washed the dishes, dried them, and put them away. He took time to collect all the shell casings and dispose of them. Now all this was not done to protect his identity as the killer. He knew that we'd know who did it. Instead, I think he did it simply because he didn't want to leave a mess. Because that's the kind of guy he was.

And some time in here he also went a little berserk, firing shots from his 9 mm automatic into the walls, floors and ceilings.

He took a shower, packed up, and then, before he left, turned on every light in the house. He got into his car, drove to Kennedy Airport, and parked in the lot. He checked into a nearby motel where, according to the desk clerks, he rarely left for the next day and a half, except to buy food and newspapers. He wouldn't even let the maid come into his room to clean up. She had to leave the towels outside the door.

There was one particularly odd thing that happened during

his stay. There was a record of his having made one phone call. Get this, he called home. Why? Beats me. Maybe he just wanted to check and see if the bodies had been found. Maybe he got homesick. Or maybe he just wanted to see if the whole thing was a bad dream. Needless to say, the call was never completed.

Wednesday evening, he took that flight to Miami.

And now we, or rather I, was on his tail.

Whatever made me think I could track Hartman down in a place where I couldn't even speak the language? That I got as far as I did was amazing.

What I was able to do was prove Hartman had been in Mexico City approximately two weeks before me, so I was actually gaining on him. At first, I haunted the bus and train stations, as well as the airport, showing his photo and a police artist's rendering of what he might look like with a beard. No luck. It would have been a chance in a million, but still, I was disheartened. With no Manny Perez to help me, a sense of being entirely alone, disconnected, overwhelmed me.

I was ready to pack it in. One more day, I promised myself. I was lying in my hotel room on what was to be my last day in Mexico when I got the bright idea of checking the local English language bookstores. I figured Hartman was a heavy reader, so maybe he'd run out of books and needed a refill. It was worth a try.

There were half a dozen English language bookstores in the city and I hit the jackpot on the third one I visited. A fellow who worked there recognized the police sketch of Hartman with a beard. He was a grubby, skuzzy-looking character with rotten teeth and scraggly gray hair tied in a ponytail. An ex-hippie, it turned out. His name was Ralph. That's it. Just Ralph. He had a last name, he said, but it defined him and according to him he was beyond defining or categorizing. "I am me," he said, "and all that that entails." He sounds like a jerk, but he was actually kind of amusing. At least he amused me. He told me he used to hang out with Jack Kerouac and William Burroughs when they lived in Mexico. When he learned I was a cop, he confided to me that he actually witnessed Burroughs shooting his wife while they played a modern-day version of William Tell Shoots the Apple Off His Son's Head. "He came this close to hitting the apple," he said, holding two fingers about an inch apart. "I think she moved when she shouldn't have."

Eventually, he got around to telling me that Hartman had been in about three weeks earlier and had picked out maybe a dozen paperback books, including some by the Latin American authors Jorge Luis Borges, Carlos Fuentes and Gabriel Garcia Marquez. Ralph, whose brains were pretty much mashed potatoes by this time—he even offered me a hit of weed, knowing I was a cop—remembered talking with Hartman but couldn't quite recall what they'd talked about, a result, I assumed, of dropping too much acid and ingesting magic mushrooms with Señors Kerouac and Burroughs. The one thing he did remember, though, was that Hartman told him he was headed south with the intention of traveling through Latin and South America. Or did this asshole just assume this to be his route because of the books Hartman bought, I asked? On second thought, he wasn't sure. It didn't matter because it made sense to me. After all, I figured Hartman wouldn't stick around Mexico City for long, especially after sending his Christmas message. He must have known we'd see it and be right on his tail. Maybe that's what he wanted.

Before leaving the bookstore I bought the same books Hartman had, thinking they might give me some kind of lead as to where he was headed, or how he was thinking. I'm not a particularly big reader, and when I do read it tends to be stuff like Grisham or Cornwall, but in this job you do what you gotta do.

Back in my hotel room, I was in a funk—depressed and frustrated. I hadn't expected to bump into Hartman on the streets of Mexico City, or drinking tequila in some neighborhood cantina, but I did think I'd get pretty close. But knowing he was lost, perhaps forever, in the wilds of South America hit me hard. I felt very out of control. I don't like to admit this to anybody, but I was tempted to hang it up. Fortunately, I didn't feel this way long because the idea of admitting failure sent shivers up my spine. Failure is not something I take kindly to. If I just persevered, I knew I'd get the break I was looking for.

On the plane back home I started to read those books Hartman had picked up. They weren't half-bad, at least the parts I could understand. But finally the stress and the hours of not sleeping got to me and I started to nod off. It was then that I had a half-sleep-induced fantasy of tracking Hartman south, from bookstore to bookstore, following a trail of incriminating books he left behind.

Jesus, I thought, as I drifted off to sleep, this thing was really beginning to get to me. And it was even getting me to read stuff I'd never, in a million years, thought I'd read.

CHAPTER THIRTY-FIVE:
JANIE MCCLELLAN

It was an impossible situation and getting worse all the time. There was no way I could continue living in Sedgewick and hold onto my sanity. I was so self-conscious that every time I stepped out of the damn house I either wore tons of clothing and a big, floppy hat so no one would recognize me. But they did. Who the fuck else would dress like that in a town like Sedgewick?

And each day at work was torture, pure torture. They looked at me as if it was my fault John turned out to be a madman, as if I turned him into a killer. They looked at me as if I was a carrier of a murder gene. And it wasn't going to change. I was branded forever with a big H on my forehead. For Hartman.

And then there was the possibility, at least in the back of my frightened, confused, pathetic little mind, of John getting in touch with me again. I mean, that Christmas card thing really freaked me out. I know I said to Floyd that I knew John would never come back, but I said that not because I believed it but because I wanted to believe it. Look, if he was still thinking about me, what would stop him from showing up one day?

I knew I could never again live what could laughingly be referred to as a normal life, but what I could do was make life a littler easier by moving the hell out of Sedgewick, out of the whole fucking state of Connecticut, in fact. So that's what I decided to do. The next step would be to break it to Charlie. I mean, I had to do it, right? To just disappear one day wouldn't have been fair. And I guess I could have asked you to do it for me . . . but that wouldn't have been fair to you, either, would it?

I thought I owed it to Floyd to tell him what I was planning, so I called him up one day. He wasn't happy about it.

"The only reason you want me to stay is because you think that someday John will come back because of me," I said.

There was a moment of silence.

"That's true, isn't it?"

"Maybe."

"So you want me to live my life for you and John."

"I'm sorry."

"You're sorry because that's what you want or you're sorry for wanting that?"

"Probably a little of both."

"Well, I'm sorry, too, because I'm going to do what I think is best for me, not for you. You'll have to do your job without me."

"Yes," he said, "I will."

CHAPTER THIRTY-SIX:
CHARLIE FLOYD

Janie McClellan was right. I was a selfish sonofabitch. But you know, maybe that's what makes me good at what I do. I'm single-minded and tenacious. I keep my eye on the prize and don't give up. After I hung up the phone with her, sure, I was a little ashamed of myself. Because sometimes I forget people have feelings. And that they have their own lives to live. The truth is, she probably was doing the right thing. For her. And the truth is, Hartman wasn't coming back. I was going to have to go out and find him. That was my job. And that's what I was going to do.

A few days later, we got a report from Interpol. Someone had reported spotting Hartman in Caracas. Every hour on the hour I called in to see if there was anything new. It wasn't until the next morning that we found out they picked up the guy and it was just someone who looked like Hartman. I was disappointed, of course, but I tried to look on the bright side. At least someone out there besides me, someone with more resources than the State of Connecticut, was still looking for him. It gave me hope that we would eventually find him.

Even with what little Janie was taking with her, it still took us the better part of a day to finish packing. When we had, six or seven cardboard boxes were stacked against the living room wall and four suitcases were lined up in the hall. Janie looked at everything, sighed, and said, "Well, there I am. All of me. Why not take all of me?"

Her plane was leaving the next morning for San Francisco and I was to send her stuff out there as soon as she found a place to settle. She was going to take a month or so to explore, she said. Drive up and down the coast until she found a place with her name on it. Then I'd get the call to ship her belongings. I didn't mind doing it. It was a way to stay in touch with her. Made me feel like I was still part of her life, even if I wasn't. But I don't mind telling you, I dreaded that phone call with the address where she wanted her stuff sent. Part of me was hoping I'd get a call telling me she hated California and was coming back. I didn't think she could run away from things.

But another part of me was glad she'd gone; glad she was out of my life. Seeing her get on that plane was almost a relief. Maybe it was because I was getting rid of one more distraction. Or maybe it was because she was a constant reminder of my failure to find Hartman.

I needed to be on my own for a while. I needed to be responsible to no one but myself.

Chapter Thirty-Seven:
Reverend Chapman

I received the letter the Friday just prior to Easter Sunday, nearly six months after the murders. I must say, the significance of that time of year was certainly not lost on me: the Resurrection.

I remember it distinctly. When I got to my office that morning there were perhaps three or four letters on my desk awaiting my attention. If I'm not mistaken, I believe it was the second one I opened. Inside, there was a plain piece of white note paper, about four by six inches in size. The message was printed in black ink in large, perfectly formed block letters. So perfect, in fact, that it was almost as if they'd been typed. It read:

Dear Reverend,

I believe I have the answer to that question we were contemplating some time ago. After giving it much thought, I believe the answer lies in a question: If there were a God, would He have allowed something like this to happen?

At first it didn't quite register since, to be perfectly honest, I hadn't thought about John Hartman in several months. After all, life goes on, doesn't it? Well, for most of us it does, no offense—because I see that you're still working on this book of yours. But for me, there was Easter and, in addition, we were in the midst of an enormous fundraising campaign. The idea was to get to church members while they were still caught up in the spirit of Easter. You might think the Christmas season is the perfect opportunity for this sort of thing, but I'm afraid you'd be wrong. People are much more involved in spending their money on Christmas gifts and, as a result, the church comes in a poor second.

It took a second reading before it dawned on me that it was a message from John. It was so bizarre. I mean, a note like this completely out of the blue. I sat there a minute and suddenly this very eerie feeling came over me. I can't quite explain it, but it was as if John was actually in the room with me, standing behind me, looking over my shoulder, laughing at me. I know it sounds ridiculous, but I could actually feel his presence. I read it over two or three times and then, realizing it might have some important clue as to his whereabouts, I set it down carefully on my desk. Then I retrieved the envelope from the trash. The postmark was Colombia, South America, and it had been mailed almost two weeks earlier.

I closed my eyes and tried to picture John sitting there in some hotel, perhaps, writing his letter, a sly smile of victory on his face because I truly believed he was getting some kind of perverse, diabolical pleasure out of taunting me. Had he, I wondered, planned and carried out this whole monstrous murder spree simply to disprove the existence of God? Was he that sick?

I didn't sit there thinking about it long. Instead, I called the Sedgewick police and was informed that the case was now being handled exclusively by the FBI and the Connecticut Department of Investigations. I called Mr. Floyd's office and within an hour and a half he was at my door.

He was the same fellow who'd interviewed me in December but I'm not sure I would have recognized him. He seemed to have lost a considerable amount of weight and his face was pale and drawn. He looked as though he'd been through some serious illness. I also seemed to recall that he was dressed rather flamboyantly the first time we met, but now his clothes had a subdued, almost funereal look. What's more, his dark, conservatively cut blue suit looked as if it could have used a good cleaning and pressing.

He didn't say much, just asked to see the letter. When I showed it to him, though, his face brightened and he got much more animated. He asked all sorts of questions, *rat-a-tat-tat*, machine gun–style, including whether this was the first time I'd heard from John since the murders. Of course it was, I said. Did he think I would hold back something as important as that? He didn't answer. He seemed to tune out for an instant. Then, just like that, he was back, asking more questions, most of which I couldn't possibly have the answers to.

Finally, when he slowed down, I asked how the investigation was progressing. He didn't seem to care much for that question. He grunted and asked if he could use the phone. I directed him to one in an adjacent office so he could have some privacy. When he returned, he said he'd have to take the letter with him. "Be my guest," I said, since I was just as happy to be rid of it . . . and him. He took it and the envelope and carefully, by the very edges, slipped them into a manila envelope he'd taken from his briefcase.

"I wish I could be more help," I said.

"So do I," he muttered.

"I hope you don't mind my saying this, but I get the distinct impression something's wrong. Is there anything I can do to help?"

He looked at me like I was some kind of madman and said, "I don't think so, Reverend." Very slowly. Articulating each word like it was its own, individual sentence. I. Don't. Think. So.

"I just thought . . . well, you know, that's what I'm here for."

"Is that what?"

I was taken aback by his tone and the edge to his voice, as though he was accusing me of something. "I get the sense you don't particularly care for me, Mr. Floyd. Am I wrong?"

"I don't know where you'd get an idea like that, Reverend. I have only the highest respect for you . . . and your profession."

"Well, frankly, your tone is a bit off-putting. If there's something I've done to offend you. Well, I certainly didn't mean anything. In fact, I was totally unaware . . ."

He rubbed his face and ran his hand through his hair. "I'm sorry if I gave you that impression, Reverend. It's got nothing to do with you. I'm just tired, is all. It's been a rough few months. I've been under a lot of pressure."

"Maybe you ought to consider taking some time off. When was the last time you had a vacation, if I may ask?"

"Can't remember."

"Well, there you have it. We all need to get away once in a while. I assume that's especially the case for someone in your line of work. Speaking of which, let me ask you something. It's been some time now and when I spoke to the folks at the Sedgewick police department earlier they told me they were no longer working on the case. I was wondering just how active the case still is, as far as you're concerned, I mean."

"Very."

"Oh, are you any closer to finding him? I mean, this has got to come to an end sometime."

"We're making progress," he said, but I knew he was lying. Or maybe just trying to convince himself.

"Well, do you think this letter will be of any help?"

He looked at the manila envelope and shrugged. "Maybe. Maybe not."

"Well, I suppose it does help at least in pinpointing where he's . . ."

"Sure. A couple of weeks ago."

"But still . . ."

"Hartman is a very clever man. He knows just what he's doing. He's not about to tell us anything he doesn't want us to know. Believe me, he's long gone from Bogotá now. He wouldn't have sent this if he didn't have plans to beat it out of there soon."

"I take it, then, your assumption is that he's in complete control of his . . . faculties."

"Yeah, we could say that."

"But perhaps he's not. Doesn't that possibility enter your mind at all?"

"I'm afraid not."

"I admire your confidence, how sure you are of yourself."

"And you're not?"

"Like most, I have my doubts. I'd be the first to admit that."

"Which brings us to the contents of the letter, doesn't it?"

"Yes . . . I suppose it does."

"Well, what do you think?"

"About the contents."

"Yes."

"Well, it's not convincing one way or the other. Lots of horrible things happen. People die every day—violent deaths, untimely deaths, disastrous deaths, inexplicable deaths. That doesn't mean there's no God. It's all in God's plan and we can't be presumptuous enough to know what that plan is, can we?"

"Actually, Reverend, I try not to concern myself with such lofty matters. They only confuse me, and I'm confused enough as it is. Sometimes I have trouble deciding what I want for dinner. But it seems to me questions like that are the bread and butter of your profession and pat answers like that might not satisfy everyone. You can understand that, can't you?"

I didn't like what I considered Mr. Floyd's attack on me.

What did he want me to tell him? That John was right? That there was no God simply because he'd gone off the deep end and killed five innocent people? Is that what he wanted? Well, that's not what he was going to get. Not from me. I didn't pretend to have all the answers and it was unfair of him to expect them from me. His job was to find John Hartman and he wasn't able to do it. Let him worry about himself first. Let he who casts the first stone and all that.

After the exchange, he left and I got back to work. I had a long list of people to call for contributions and I was only halfway through. I hope there wouldn't be any more silly interruptions.

CHAPTER THIRTY-EIGHT:
JOHN HARTMAN

André Gide said it. "Please don't understand me too quickly."

But people do it all the time. They think they understand, but they don't. They just don't. They never look beneath the surface. They see what they want to see. They hear what they want to hear. They are quick to judge. Judge not, lest you be judged. It's a cliché. But clichés are real. They originally had meaning. But now they are clichés because all meaning has been wrung out of them.

I am real. But all meaning has been wrung out of me, too. I want people to forget me. To forget that I ever existed. That's what I want to do. Forget I ever existed. I'm not there yet. But I will be.

And yet I need to be understood. Because if you understand me. If you can understand me. Then perhaps you can understand yourself. I must forget myself, but you must not. Because there are others like me. And if you can understand me, perhaps you can understand them. And if you understand me and you understand them, perhaps something like this can be stopped before it happens. If I felt I had choices, other choices, I would not have done what I did. I would not have become the monster I was.

But that will change. It has changed.

I am not a monster now. I will not be a monster in the future. And so, I cannot be forgotten.

Chapter Thirty-Nine:
Charlie Floyd

Nine months had passed since the murders and my boss finally realized I'd hit a wall and so he offered me a nice, juicy murder case, something that happened in the very swank bedroom community of Westport. A couple married only a short time—he was a lawyer, she was a stockbroker—both from well-respected, upper-class families, had been brutally tortured, cigarette burns and all, then murdered in their new $3 million beachfront house. There were no signs of a break-in, no apparent motive for murder. On paper, at least, it looked good for at least a few weeks of investigation. Unfortunately, it didn't turn out that way. It was a case of premature ejaculation: all delivery and very little pleasure. No more than a day after I was on the case it broke of its own accord. One of our informants tipped us to the murderer. It turned out to be nothing more spectacular than a drug deal gone sour. The couple, dabbling in the use and sale of coke, burned a buyer who, in turn, came back for revenge. Why people like them would stoop to dealing drugs and try to pull a fast one to boot beats me, but those things happen. Kicks, I suppose. Stupid. Just plain stupid. I couldn't help thinking they deserved what they got; not like the Hartman family. It wasn't even one of my snitches who came through and so, less than two days after being assigned to the case, I was gone, back into my black hole again.

I took stock and figured the only way I was going to be able to lift myself from my depression was to get back in the thick of it again. It had been a good three months since we'd had any kind of new lead, so I decided to recharge my batteries by paying a visit to the scene of the crime.

It was a dreary, gray, threatening day in late March. The little snow left on the ground was melting fast, so the streets were wet and the ground soft and mushy. On what used to be the Hartman property someone had started building a new house, situated far back from the street, several yards away from where the original house had been. They hadn't gotten very far. By the time I got there in the late afternoon, the workers had already knocked off for the day, leaving behind the skeleton of the new frame of the house along with some building equipment, wheelbarrows, and a bulldozer scattered about the property. I parked my car and began walking across the lawn, my feet squishing into the soft ground.

When I reached the spot where the old house had been— now only the remnants of a foundation filled with dirt from the new site—I stood there with my eyes closed, trying to imagine what the house had looked like before having been destroyed by fire. I had no trouble. I knew that house as well as I knew my own. Then I tried to imagine Hartman inside, following him through the house as he committed the murders. But I couldn't quite get him in focus. So I took his photograph out of my wallet and stared at it for a long time. When I finally thought I had him committed to memory again, I closed my eyes.

It worked. I could actually see him moving purposely through the house, carrying sleeping bodies into the ballroom, laying them side by side on blankets he'd prepared earlier, aiming the pistol at their heads, pulling the trigger. Once. Twice. Three. Four. Five. Times. Murdering them one by one. I watched as he slowly climbed the stairs to his mother's room. I watched as he killed her, too; then the dog. I watched as he cleaned up, got into his car and drove off to the airport. I watched as he checked into the motel. I watched as he boarded the plane for Miami. I followed him, like a fly on his shoulder, for as far as we'd traced him. Things began to blur in my mind and soon it was as if I was the one making the journey, not Hartman. I was getting on the plane, not him. I was screwing a hooker, getting a janitorial job in Hollywood. I'd gotten myself into such a state that I felt as if I was a part of him. We were one and the same. I found myself thinking like him, acting like him or rather acting like I thought he'd act, planning his next move. And, as I stood there staring out into space, being John Hartman, it was as if he was standing there beside me, monitoring my thoughts, correcting me at every turn, saying yes, that's the way it happened, or no, that's not it at all.

A car drove up and broke the trance. Someone got out and started toward me.

"Hey, this is private property," he called out.

When he got closer I recognized him as the neighbor who'd made the initial report of trouble at the Hartman house. He didn't recognize me. He came right up, got in my face, looked me right in the eye and said, "You can't be here."

"That so?"

"Yes. This is private property. You're trespassing."

"I don't think so," I said, though I made absolutely no move to identify myself.

"I'll call the cops."

I shrugged. "Do what you have to do."

He looked harder at me. "You look familiar. Do I know you?"

"Maybe so."

"From where?"

"I'm Charles Floyd, Connecticut Department of Criminal Investigation."

"Oh. Sure. That's right. It's the beard that threw me off. I'm sorry about this, but you don't much look like a cop, and around here we all watch out for each other. Especially after . . . well, you know . . ."

"Yeah, well, that's okay. Better safe than sorry." Asshole, I wanted to add.

"Right. Well, what are you doing here?"

"Just looking around."

"Is there something new on the case, maybe?"

"Afraid not."

"Too bad. I don't think anybody here's going to have a full night's sleep until he's caught."

"Yeah, well, sooner or later . . ."

"So what are you doing here then?"

"I told you, just looking around." I couldn't keep the edge out of my voice. I was getting pissed. I didn't much appreciate the cross-examination by some nosy neighbor. I didn't have to answer to him. In the mood I was in, I didn't have to answer to anybody. But I tried to cool it. I didn't want him calling Ed and complaining and trust me, he looked like the type who would do just that. "I was in the neighborhood and thought I'd take another look around."

"Not much to see, is there? Would you like to come over for coffee or a drink, maybe?"

So he could pump me for some more information? "I don't think so, but thanks anyway. I've got to be going."

"It's going to be a beauty, you know."

"What is?"

"The new house they're putting up. Lots of money there. They're going to make it a real showplace. You know, it wasn't such a bad thing that the house burned down. It's not likely anyone around here is going to forget what happened, but having that house standing certainly wouldn't have helped matters any."

"No, I don't suppose it would." I started to walk back to my car. He followed me, close at my heels.

"You know," he said, "sometimes at night, late at night, I find myself staring out my window. I can't seem to get those lights out of my mind. Don't know if I ever will. You know, I've never told anyone this, not even my wife, but if I were to be completely honest, I'd have to admit that that thing was the highlight of my life. I know it's a terrible thing to say. I know it. But it's the truth. It's not like I wished it to happen or anything like that. But it was something, wasn't it? I feel terrible about it. I mean, if I had any control over things it never would have happened. But it did. And I still think about it, even during the day. I play it over and over in my mind. What do you think of that, Mr. Floyd?"

"I'm no shrink."

"I don't know what to make of it. I really don't. And while I'm at it, I have another admission to make. There's a part of me that doesn't want him to ever be caught. Sounds horrible, doesn't it? I mean, he ought to be caught. He's got to be caught. But there's this little part of me that says, 'Please, don't let him be caught. Let things stay the way they are.' Why do you think that is?"

I opened the car door and slid behind the wheel. "I don't know," I said. "I don't think I'm the right one to ask." I closed the door and started up the engine. He just stood there, watching me with this bewildered look on his face. He really didn't get it. Later, when I thought about it, and I did, I felt sorry for him. But at that moment I felt nothing but hatred for him and everyone else in that town like him. Imagine, my life being as messed up as it was because of John Hartman, because he was still on the loose, and here's this small-minded idiot hoping Hartman stays on the loose, just so he can feel self-important, feel alive. It was all I could to do stop from pulling out my revolver and nailing him right there, right on the edge of the

Hartman property. Now that would have been something, wouldn't it?

On the way home, I kept thinking I had to make something happen—if only to put that little man right back into the world he belonged in. I didn't know how, but I had to do something. I couldn't just sit there with my finger up my ass waiting for Hartman to "give" us something again. I had to take control.

But what the hell could I do?

CHAPTER FORTY:
JAMES KIRKLAND

I woke up early one beautiful spring morning and got dressed to meet the boys for a golf date at the club. I stepped outside to get the morning paper and noticed someone had scribbled graffiti on the curb across the street, right in front of what used to be the Hartman house. I tossed the newspaper back inside and crossed the street to get a better look. As I got closer I saw it wasn't just some inane saying or random design, but three words painted boldly in white:

JOHN HARTMAN LIVES!

Damn kids, I thought. What a sick idea for a joke. I went back inside, mad as hell, got myself a pail of soap and water, a brush and some paint remover, and started to go back outside when my wife, who was just coming down the stairs, still dressed in her bathrobe, stopped me.

"Where are you going with that stuff? I thought you were on your way to the club."

"I was, but there's something I've got to do first."

"What?"

"Some kids painted the sidewalk across the street."

"So?"

"So, I'm going to clean it up."

"Why you?"

"Someone's got to do it."

She shook her head and wrapped her robe more tightly around herself as she walked toward me and then on into the kitchen. "You know, Jim," she said, stopping at the doorway and turning to face me, "things are getting to the point where it's worse around here than it is in the city. Mary Herbert told me the other day that a bunch of kids broke into the high school, smashed some windows, threw papers all over the place, then stole a whole bunch of supplies. It's all so destructive and utterly pointless. I don't know what this world's coming to."

"Neither do I. The social fabric seems to be totally unraveling."

"I think you ought to call the police."

"I don't."

"Why not?"

"Because I can handle it."

"You always think you can handle things . . . Why don't you just toddle off to your golf game and I'll send one of the kids out to clean it up. Or I'll just do it myself."

"I don't think you should do that."

"Why not?"

"Because it's not something that's going to please you."

"Jim, what in God's name are you talking about? The whole idea of our neighborhood being defaced by graffiti artists doesn't please me. I suppose it's just some kids' idea of a harmless prank."

"I'm afraid it might be a little more malicious than that."

"What do you mean?"

"It says, 'John Hartman Lives!' "

She put her hand to her mouth in one of those ultra-dramatic, totally meaningless gestures that sometimes drive me up a wall, shook her head and said, "Oh, God, will it never end?"

"Sometime, I suppose."

"Well, not soon enough for me. Why in the world would someone do something as sick as that?"

I shrugged and looked at my watch. "Well, it's getting late.

The boys will be waiting. Tee-off time's eight-forty-six. I'd better get out there and clean it up."

"Jim . . . you don't think . . ."

"Don't be silly."

"You didn't let me finish."

"I know what you were going to say and it's ridiculous. Just ridiculous. It's kids, that's all. Let's not turn this into something more sinister than it is."

"It was just a thought. Too bad Eleanor doesn't come on weekends, or else she could clean it up."

I went outside and cleaned up the mess myself and, as I did, it reminded me I ought to give a call to the cops to find out if there had been any new developments in the case. But I'd make sure I didn't speak to that Mr. Floyd. I just didn't like him. And frankly, I think the feeling was mutual. There's a lot of resentment around here. It's a class thing, I'm afraid. People don't realize we're all in the same boat, you know.

I'd give the Chief of Police a call. First thing Monday morning. That's what I'd do.

In the meantime, though, I had to reassure my wife and everyone else that there was absolutely no chance John Hartman was back in town.

CHAPTER FORTY-ONE:
PETER SIMPSON

We met on a train, just like in that classic Hitchcock film with Robert Walker and Farley Granger.

It was the local from Guatemala City to San Salvador. I was traveling through Latin America by bus and rail trying to soak up local color and gather information for a book I was working on. I thought since I didn't seem to be getting anywhere with freelance magazine writing, despite the fact that I was always kept busy, I ought to tackle something big, something significant—kind of like what you're doing. In fact, we're very similar that way I guess. Besides, I needed something to shake up my life. Fact is, I was having trouble at home. My wife and I were getting to the stage where we were talking about our relationship more than we were living it, a sure sign we were in trouble. I blamed it on the never-ending anxiety my lifestyle produced: never knowing when the next check was coming in; never knowing what I was doing next; always groping for the next story idea; and, maybe most of all, the lack of continuity, just one short assignment after another. You know what I mean, since you've been through it, too.

So I cooked up the idea for a book, a book that would take me away from home for a while, so my wife and I could have some alone time, away from our everyday problems, our everyday confrontations. A chance to get our feelings sorted out. The idea I finally settled on was a book about conditions in Latin America, focusing exclusively on the social rather than the political, which is a Pandora's box I didn't want to open. Unfortunately, after only a few weeks on the road I was finding that the two were inexorably intertwined. At the moment I met him I was grappling with this problem, which was playing havoc with my original plan for the book. I was even giving serious thought to calling the whole thing off. But the bottom line was, I'd gone too far to throw in the towel. Too many other people were involved. Too many other people were depending on me. Too many other people had made sacrifices so I could get my life back together. I'd created a kind of consortium, with investors like my parents, my brother, my wife, her parents, several friends, not to mention my agent.

After procrastinating a while I used the borrowed money to take two months off from trying to get any new magazine assignments and work up a proposal I thought would sell. Then I held my breath and handed it over to my agent. She liked it, though she suggested a few changes, which I managed quickly enough. Then I held my breath while she circulated it. It was rejected from five different houses. I became depressed and morose, adding yet another strain to our already faltering marriage. My wife was sympathetic, but I could see she was at the end of her patience. Every morning she'd go off to work leaving me sitting on the couch watching TV. Every evening she'd return and find me in precisely the same position. I knew she was getting pissed, rightfully so, but it was almost as if I wanted to see just how much I could get away with. I was even getting a perverse pleasure out of seeing how long I could keep it up.

It turned out to be the lucky sixth. An editor thought enough of the idea to give me a contract and I was advanced enough dough to keep me going through Latin America for two or three months, if I traveled like a peasant, which was the point anyway. I had little in savings but, with a book contract in hand, it was easy enough to scrounge up a few thousand more from relatives and friends, which enabled me to stretch my time in Latin America to six months. No more days on the couch watching TV. Every so often, my wife would fly down to be with me. The rest of the time we'd have a paid vacation from each other to try to settle our differences.

For someone as undisciplined as I am, someone used to spending no more than a few weeks at a time on a project, it was a challenge. It was frightening but exhilarating, and I began to think of it as a way to test my mettle, to find out what I was really made of. My weapons were over two dozen notebooks in which I scribbled non-stop, along with a dozen pens, and a tape recorder into which I tried to speak cogent, witty and important observations, most of which, by the way, seemed ridiculously banal when I played them back. But everything I did for those six months was supposed to feed into my work.

I'd been in Latin America almost a month when I met a man who called himself John Evans. He was sitting half a dozen seats in front of me, the only other gringo on a train filled mostly with local peasants traveling from one small village on the line to another. It was a decrepit wooden milk train, hot and virtually airless. I was disoriented and out of sorts. I hadn't spoken English to anyone in nearly a week and I was beginning to lose my sense of identity. I needed a shower badly and I needed companionship even more. Finally, after watching him for more than half an hour, I approached and asked if he minded if I sat down. He said no. He looked to be in his late forties, early fifties. He had a short, dark beard, sprinkled with gray. His hair was scraggly and uncombed. He wore tan slacks and a blue polo shirt with the collar turned in. A handkerchief was wrapped around his neck. A small brown suitcase was on the rack above his head and a Delta Airlines flight bag was at his feet.

I sat down next to him and introduced myself. He did the same. He didn't look well. He was pale and drawn with deep lines etched in his face. I asked if he'd been sick. He said he'd been having trouble with his stomach. Join the crowd, I said. I told him not to worry, that he'd get used to it, that his body would eventually build up antibodies and that soon he'd be eating like a native. I told him what I was doing and asked where he was headed.

"South America," he said.

"There are easier ways," I said.

"I suppose."

"Why this way, then?"

"Because it's different."

"It's different, all right. You're an adventurous man, Mr. Evans. I'll say that for you. Exactly where is it you're headed?"

He hesitated a moment, like he wasn't quite sure, and then said, "I thought I'd probably end up in Argentina."

"Why Argentina?"

He looked at me through heavy-lidded, dark-circled eyes. "You ask a lot of questions."

"I know. Force of habit. I apologize. I suppose it's my way of making a connection with people. I'm not too good with small talk, you see, or with people in general. My wife's always kidding me about that. She says she always knows where to find me at a party. Either by the food or alone in a corner, watching everybody else have a good time. You know, it's funny, but most people are under the impression journalists are outgoing. Generally speaking, I don't think that's the case. Mostly, we're a bashful lot. Curious, but bashful. I'm always self-conscious when I meet new people, so I tend to ask a lot of questions. Some of them might be construed as being invasive, I guess. It's a form of self-protection, I guess. Anyway, I don't mind if when I'm asking a question that cuts too close to the bone someone just says, 'none of your damn business.' Just so it's done in a nice way. As it is, I'm probably turning red. So, I'll just take it that my question about Argentina is one of those questions to which the answer is, 'none of your damn business.' "

"It's all right," he said, removing the handkerchief from his neck to wipe his brow. He tied it back around his neck and said, "It's appropriate, I think. I've had some trouble at home and I decided to take off . . ."

"So you're running away from home. Join the club."

"Running away from home. Yes, I guess." He looked me in the eye without blinking. His eyes were deep brown and focused on me so sharply that I had to look away. It was as if he was trying to look inside me, inside my soul. "It's where all the fugitives go, isn't it?"

"Yes. I suppose it is. But tourists, too. You don't mean you're literally a fugitive, do you?"

He didn't answer me directly. Instead, he said as he turned away from me to look out the window, "Sometimes I feel like a Nazi war criminal. Like Mengele or Borman. Argentina . . . that's where they . . ." His voice trailed off and he continued to stare out the window.

I thought this was a rather startling statement and wanted to know more about him. Yet I sensed I had to be gentle with him if I wanted to learn more. He was obviously disturbed, but not crazy disturbed. With this in mind, I widened the scope of my questions, trying to get him to talk about himself without being aware of how much he was telling me. I also did something I'm not particularly proud of, something I'd like to think I did from habit. I surreptitiously flipped on my recorder, which was in my pocket.

"Where you from originally?"

"Chicago."

"The Windy City."

"That's right."

" 'I am an American, Chicago born—Chicago, that somber city . . .' "

" '. . . and go at things as I have taught myself, free-style, and will make the record in my own way: first to knock, first admitted; sometimes an innocent knock, sometimes a not so innocent. But a man's character is his fate, says Heraclitus, and in the end there isn't any way to disguise the nature of the knocks by acoustical work on the door or gloving the knuckles.' "

"Hey, so you're a Bellow fan, too."

"Among others." He continued to stare out the window, but now he was wringing his hands.

"And you're from Chicago, huh? I've been there a few times. In fact, I once wrote a piece on old man Wrigley. Not a Cubs fan by chance?"

"When I was a kid. Not now."

"Yeah, well, that was the time for it, I suppose. When you're a kid you can put up with losers almost indefinitely. When you grow up, though, and there's not that much time left to hope for big improvements, it's another story. Sometimes, you switch to a winner or just abandon the loser. Maybe that's what's wrong with this country. We're all looking for winners. Like Lombardi said, 'Winning isn't everything, it's the only thing.' Still have family in Chicago?"

"They're all gone."

"You mean like to other parts of the country?"

"Uh, yeah."

"Married?"

"Not anymore."

"I notice you're still wearing a wedding band."

"Habit," he said, twisting the ring, which seemed too large for his finger.

"Gotcha. Maybe that's the kind of trouble you were talking about when you said you were running away . . ."

"I didn't say I was running away . . ."

"You're right. That's what I said."

I decided to give it a rest. I could see he didn't feel like talking anymore, so I switched off my recorder. He leaned back, started fanning himself with a paperback copy of *One Hundred Years of Solitude*, and stared out the window. We were moving along the coast and you could see the Pacific, calm and inviting. It was so bloody hot I just wished we could stop a while and take a quick swim. The train moved slowly, but it did keep moving. The only relief we got came when a vendor selling fresh fruit came through the car. I stopped him and picked out some ripe mangoes and bananas for the two of us to share, but Evans wouldn't let me pay for them. "My treat," he said. "Save your money for research." He pulled out a wad of pesos and overpaid. When I pointed this out to him, he shrugged and said, "So what?"

I didn't feel I could press him for any more information about himself without getting him to trust me first, so I started telling him about myself. My work, the problems I was having with the book, my problems with my wife. He seemed to listen attentively, sucking on a mango, mostly just nodding his head. I was talking about myself, but what I really wanted to know was about him.

At one point, I pulled out some snapshots of my family, but he shied away from looking at them. When I showed him one of my father with fishing poles in our hands and the day's catch at our feet, he began to tear up.

"Something wrong?"

He shook his head and wiped his eyes with his handkerchief.

"I'm sorry," I said.

"Nothing to be sorry about. My father is dead." And that was that.

Evans's vulnerability is what drew me to him. But something

else drew me to him as well: the secrets he was keeping. And I knew he had secrets. I knew he was holding back, hiding something big, terrible even, and that that was probably the reason he was on that train, traveling south, away from trouble, in much the same way I was.

The brick wall he'd built up around himself seemed impregnable. I didn't think I had nearly enough time to break through it, or if I ever could. Yet I couldn't give up. I knew a good story when I saw one. So when the train finally pulled into San Salvador late in the afternoon, I invited him to have a drink with me at my hotel.

"I don't think so," he said politely as he hoisted his airline bag over his shoulder, picked up his suitcase and walked unsteadily toward the exit to the train.

"Hell, why not? Two gringos on the loose in a foreign country ought to stick together, don't you think? Besides, I'm enjoying your company."

"I'm very tired and I'd like to get some rest. As you can see, I haven't been well lately. I'm sure you understand."

"Yeah. Of course. But maybe later this evening."

"That's a possibility."

"You'll be here for a while, then?"

"I think so."

"Great. I'll catch up with you later. In the meantime, thanks for the fruit and the conversation."

"You're welcome," he said, and then he walked off toward the center of town while I stuck around the station for a while longer, loading up on train schedules and trying to pick up some advice from a few of the locals as to the best way to get from here to there. When I'd finished and was walking to my hotel I suddenly realized I'd neglected to find out where Evans was staying. I checked my hotel when I got there to see if he had a reservation, but he didn't.

I could have let it go, but I didn't. The next morning, after breakfast, I began canvassing all the hotels in town, looking for him. I had to speak to him again. I had to find out what his story was. Finally, with hotels running out, I found the right one. Unfortunately, he'd checked out very early that morning. I rushed to the train station to see if he'd gotten on an early train. The ticket seller, a sleepy fellow who was reading a football magazine, told me no one of that description had bought a ticket that morning. So I checked the bus depot. Same story. It was almost as if he'd just disappeared off the face of the earth. The only explanation I could come up with was that he'd walked, hitchhiked or taken a cab out of the city, only to pick up the train at some small village down the line.

He haunted me all that day and the next. So much so, I couldn't get any of my own work done. I kept wondering about him. Who he really was. What he was running from. What he'd done. I don't know why, but for the next two days I walked the streets of San Salvador, thinking I might bump into him.

And for the next month or so, whenever I reached another village, I'd ask about the mysterious gringo with a beard carrying a suitcase and an airline flight bag. But no one seemed to have seen him but me.

Chapter Forty-Two:
Judy Hartman Swanson

"It's you, isn't?" My hands shook and my heart pounded in my chest.

"I know it's you, John, so you might as well speak up."

He didn't hang up, like the other times. All I could hear was breathing. Steady, rhythmic breathing, like in the hospital shows when they're doing an operation. It was the third phone call I'd received in the last three weeks. They were all the same. They came in the afternoon when I was the only one in the house. The phone would ring, I'd pick it up and say hello, but no one would answer. I'd say hello again, and then there'd be this click and the line would go dead. This time, though, after two hellos, he was still there. I knew it was John. I could feel it in my stomach. I knew his silences. I grew up with them.

"Well, John, I'm waiting."

I heard a whispered voice. I couldn't make it out. "You'll have to speak up, John. I can hardly hear you."

In a very soft voice I heard, "Are you tapped?"

I was getting angry and impatient with him. "How would I know, John? Do you think they'd bother tapping my phone for a whole year? I think almost everybody's forgotten about you, John. Now why are you calling? What do you want from me?"

There was silence and then he said, in a voice so strained and so thin I hardly recognized it, "I don't know."

"Well, I certainly don't."

Silence.

"This is ridiculous, John. What do you want? Tell me, so we can get this over with." I was so nervous I could hardly speak. A voice inside me kept saying, "Hang up. Hang up." But I couldn't.

Finally, he said, "How are you?" in a voice that seemed to be stretched out of shape, if you can possibly understand what I mean.

"How do you think I am? You killed my mother, John. You killed my niece and nephews. You killed my sister-in-law. You even killed the damn dog!" I was almost crying now, but I held myself back because I didn't want to give him the satisfaction. "My only living blood relative other than my kids is a murderer. That's how I am. Listen, John, this has to stop. You've been gone for a year now and I think it ought to stay that way. Have you no shame, John? Have you no shame?"

He didn't say anything for what seemed like several minutes. But I wasn't going to hang up. I wanted him to suffer. Finally, he said, "That's all I have . . ."

"So what do you want from me?"

"Aren't you going to ask where I am?"

"No. Frankly, I don't want to know. Because if I did know I'd turn you in in a New York minute."

"Do you think I ought to give myself up?"

"No. As a matter of fact, I think that's the last thing in the world I want you to do. I don't want you dredging it all up again. You think it's been easy for me? It wasn't, John. Damn you. I was hounded for months. By police. By reporters. By friends. By neighbors. How do you think I explained to my kids that my brother, their uncle, was a murderer? That their uncle murdered their grandmother? I might as well have been the murderer, John . . ." I couldn't help myself. I started to cry. "I don't want to have to go through that again. You've done enough harm, John, and I don't think your coming back and turning yourself in would do anyone any good, except maybe you. And to be brutally honest, John, I'd rather see you live with what you've done. It's obvious you're not having an easy time of it, and that's fine with me."

"Don't you want to know why I did it?"

"No. No, I don't. There's no why as far as I'm concerned. If you give me a why, that's just a way of condoning what you did. No rationalization. No explanation. I just want you to hang up and I don't ever want to hear from you again. Do you hear me? NEVER."

"You're my sister . . ." he whined.

"And that was your mother, your wife and your children you murdered. You bastard. You dirty bastard. That was my mother . . ." I couldn't control myself any longer. Tears were streaming down my face. "I hate you. I hate you," I shouted into the phone and then, when all I could hear was breathing, I slammed the phone down.

I had to sit there for a good fifteen minutes before I was finally able to compose myself. I didn't tell anyone about John's call—you're the first one. I wished him dead. I prayed for him to die, alone, anonymous. And maybe then I'd be free of it.

CHAPTER FORTY-THREE:
CHARLIE FLOYD

I had the fucking paper right in front of me and there it was in black and white, but I still couldn't fucking believe it.

Move to Declare Connecticut Killer Legally Dead

State authorities are now petitioning the courts in Connecticut to declare John Hartman legally deceased. Two years ago this past November, Hartman, aged 48, disappeared from his Sedgewick, Ct., home at the same time that five members of his family—his wife, Adele, 45, his sons, Edward, 16, Paul, 13, and daughter, Kathy, 15, and his mother, Helen, 71—were found slain, each shot once in the head, in their 19-room mansion at 541 Oakdale Drive. Police have been searching for Hartman, a prime suspect in the case, since that time . . .

I was livid. I grabbed the paper and burst into Ed's office. "What the hell's going on here?"

"Easy, Charles. Have a seat and relax."

"I don't want to relax. I want to know who the hell's behind this," I sputtered, banging my fist on poor Ed's desk. "And why the hell wasn't I informed?"

"Several of the good citizens of Sedgewick, that's who. They don't much like the idea of this thing hanging over their heads for eternity. They want to get rid of the stigma once and for all. And I don't think it's such a bad idea. Chances are the guy's not with us anymore. I mean, give me a break. Nothing in two years. Nada. You know as well as I do he probably killed himself very quietly somewhere. Conscience is a funny thing, Charles, it never really sleeps."

"Fuck that shit. This guy's not like that. He has no conscience. He's disassociated himself from what he did. He has no remorse. And God knows how many other people he's iced when he's found himself in a tight spot."

"You're being unreasonable. If this guy is alive, and I doubt it, and if he's killed anyone else, chances are it's caught up to him. You know, nine times out of ten that's the case. A guy robs a liquor store, he's not caught, so he robs another one. Eventually, the law of averages catches up with him. He gets caught. No one gets away with anything forever."

"You're obviously a religious man, Ed, but I'm not. I'm going to fight this."

"Lots of luck. I don't know why in God's name this is so important to you. It's not as though if the guy turns up one day he won't be caught and prosecuted. We don't stop looking—it goes into our cold case file, but the case isn't closed. There's no statute of limitations on murder. You know that as well as I do. So why put up such a fuss?"

"It's the goddamn principle."

He shook his head and tapped a pencil on the side of the desk. "No, I think it's a lot more than that, and if you look deep inside yourself you'd agree. You always did take this case too personally. Maybe deep down you identify with this guy and maybe that scares the hell out of you."

"That's crazy."

"Is it? Well, maybe it is, if you say so. But I do know that what is crazy is this obsession of yours. Let go of it. Pull yourself together. They're going to declare Hartman legally dead whether you like it or not, and I think maybe you ought to, too."

"I can't do that."

"Why not?"

"Because I know he's out there. And I know another thing, too. I know one day he's coming back. He's going to waltz into the center of Sedgewick. He won't be able to help himself. It's like those letters he sent Janie McClellan and the Reverend. He's connected here like he is no place else and his life won't ever be complete until he returns and closes the circle. And Ed, when he does come back, I'm gonna be here."

"That's fine, Charles. I think it's ruining your life, but it's yours to ruin. You don't see it, but you're as much of a fugitive as he is. Maybe more, because he might be dead. You want to sit around waiting for him, fine. But in the meantime, this thing is going through and if I were you I'd just sit back and smile, like it means absolutely nothing, which is exactly what it does mean. There's no sense giving yourself a heart attack over what's nothing more than a symbolic gesture. Go home, have a couple of beers, then take Jennifer, or whatever the name of your latest girl is, out to dinner and a movie."

That's a stupid thing to say, I thought, but for a change I kept my mouth shut. Then, realizing I must be coming off a raving lunatic, I said, "I'm sorry about the way I barged in here, Ed."

"Don't apologize. I've known you too damn long not to understand a little of what's going on up there. We've all gone through it one time or another. It's like a love affair gone bad. Sometimes, it's tough to let go."

"Yeah, well, it's been two years now. I'm not so sure the wound's going to heal."

"Time, Charles. Time will take care of it. Trust me on this one. Have I ever been wrong?"

"All the time, Ed. All the time."

Chapter Forty-Four:
Dr. Lawson

The patient came in sometime shortly after Thanksgiving. He complained of a series of ailments, including a bad cold—which I subsequently diagnosed as Type A strain flu—severe migraine headaches and insomnia. In addition, his face and torso were bruised in several locations and he had some facial abrasions just below the left eye and on both cheeks. These injuries looked to be less than a week old.

He informed me that his name was John Evans and that he was passing through San Antonio on his way to visit relatives in Corpus Christi. He looked to be in his mid to late forties and was casually dressed in a rumpled white button-down shirt, navy blue blazer, and wrinkled tan slacks. When I asked by whom he'd been referred, he said he'd simply been walking down the street and had seen my sign outside.

We spoke for a few minutes first, small talk mainly, but he seemed rather agitated and anxious for the examination to begin. I suggested that since he had several complaints I give him a complete physical. He was agreeable. I asked if he had medical insurance and he said he did not. He indicated that he would pay in cash.

While I went into an adjacent room to finish with another patient, Mr. Evans filled out a personal medical history form. When I returned, I glanced over it and found nothing out of the ordinary. He had not, however, named a family physician and when I asked him about this he said he had none. That he'd passed away.

All told, I saw him a total of perhaps forty-five minutes and these were my findings:

The patient was five feet eleven inches tall and weighed 154 pounds, well within the prescribed healthy limits for a man his age and build. When I informed him of these statistics, however, he said they must be wrong. He insisted he was a bit over six feet and weighed 165 pounds. I was certain of my measurements, yet to avoid problems, I re-measured and re-weighed the patient and came up with the same figures. He seemed perplexed.

He had a small build-up of wax in both ears, but it was certainly nothing of any serious medical consequence. His nasal passages were, of course, clogged as a result of his flu, and his chest cavity was congested for the same reason. As I said, Mr. Evans was suffering from a severe case of the flu accompanied by cold symptoms, for which I suggested bed rest, plenty of liquids and aspirin. For his migraine headaches, which I surmised were due to tension rather than any particular physical manifestation, I prescribed a mild dosage of Fiornal. As far as his insomnia was concerned, under pressure from him I prescribed Ambien, but suggested he use it only if he felt it absolutely necessary, as I don't like to see my patients become dependent upon drugs to induce sleep.

Otherwise, I found his heartbeat to be regular and strong, his lungs in relatively good condition. But his blood pressure was borderline high and I suggested he cut down on his salt intake. In general, he seemed to be lacking in proper nourishment and, when I questioned him about his diet, he admitted that he'd been eating mostly junk food while on the road. I cautioned him against this and suggested he introduce more fruits and vegetables into his diet.

Mr. Evans seemed extremely agitated throughout the

examination and I suspected he might be suffering from a mild case of exhaustion and nervous tension. I even suggested he might consider a short stay in the hospital until he got back on his feet again, but he rejected this notion vehemently, saying it was important that he reach Corpus Christi by the next evening. I asked him specifically about his cuts and bruises, which I treated with an iodine solution after making certain there was no infection. But he refused to give me a satisfactory explanation as to how he received them. I believe he mumbled something about falling down a flight of stairs, which I found highly unlikely. Looked more like the kinds of injuries he might sustain in a fight.

When the examination was completed, my nurse presented him with a bill, which included a blood test, the results of which he never received. He paid in full in cash, thanked me, asked for the address of the nearest pharmacy, and that was the last I saw of him.

In retrospect, I suppose it should have been obvious that this was a man who was under a serious emotional strain, but it's difficult, when you see a patient only once and know virtually nothing about him, to pick up intangibles like that. Besides, it was the onset of the flu season and several of my regular patients were lined up in my outer office for their flu shots. As far as I was concerned, he was just another transient passing through on his way someplace else.

The blood test?

Oh, yes. Well, he never saw the results, but he was a little anemic and his cholesterol count, as I recall, was quite high, high enough for him to be concerned. I definitely would have him on medication and suggested a lifestyle change.

CHAPTER FORTY-FIVE:
JOHN HARTMAN

"Hey, Richie, we're gonna head over to Ruby Tuesday's after work for a burger and a couple beers. Wanna join us?"

"I'm kinda swamped, Larry . . ."

"Come on, man. All work and no play . . ."

"I don't know . . ."

"Come on, man. Just an hour or two." Larry leaned in close to me. "Who's gonna know? Who's gonna care?"

"You're the devil, Larry."

"That's me, man. The goddamn, motherfuckin' devil. Besides, what have you got waiting for you at home?"

"Nothing."

"Yeah. Nothing."

"And what have you got waiting for you over at Ruby Tuesday's?"

"Fun."

"That's the secret word, Richie."

He was right. I was footloose and fancy free. I could go out, if I wanted to. I could have fun, if I wanted to. The work could wait. My boss loved me. And why shouldn't he? Who worked harder than I did? Who came in earlier and stayed later than I did? I had been in and out of the country and I preferred in, and so I had returned to the States and settled in Phoenix. A place of dry heat. A place where I was building a new life.

I was Richie.

I pulled out a folder and tucked the papers I was working on into it.

"That's my man," Larry said, patting me on my shoulder.

I put the folder into a desk drawer, grabbed my jacket from behind my chair, and followed him out the door.

A burger and a beer sounded pretty good to me.

CHAPTER FORTY-SIX:
CHARLIE FLOYD

Last week, I got a postcard from Janie McClellan. She's moved again. This time to San Diego. I hadn't heard from her in almost a year, but she never failed to inform me of her new addresses. And she moved around a lot. I hadn't seen or spoken to her in a couple of years, but we kept in touch via email. She was married a while, but it didn't work out. I was glad when I heard because it meant that she was at least trying to get on with her life. I knew it wasn't easy. It never is for victims. And that's what she was. A victim. Several times during the past couple years I'd been tempted to give her a call, but each time I held back. Why open up old wounds for her? And it was really just a way for me to grasp at straws, to keep my finger in the pie, so to speak. She was really the only link to Hartman. It was this weird triangle, me and Hartman and Janie McClellan. She had a need to stay in touch with me, and I with her, because both of us were tied together by Hartman. Life is weird, isn't it?

Anyway, it seemed now that she'd moved again and had taken a job as a private secretary to some corporate big shot. Big bucks, she said. I whipped off an email, congratulating her on her new job. For the rest of the day, after I sent the email, I was in a funk, thinking maybe I shouldn't have sent it at all. Maybe it was up to me to sever the connection because as long as I was still in the picture, as long as John Hartman was still out there someplace, neither she nor I could ever live peacefully.

CHAPTER FORTY-SEVEN:
CHARLIE FLOYD

I still believe in myself. It isn't easy after years of frustration and failure, but I do. What's more, I still believe in my own power. I'm still good at what I do. I'm a craftsman, okay. I know all the tricks of the trade and I'm willing to use whatever's available, whatever will get the job done. But, like I said, first and foremost I believe in my own power and ability, and that's probably why using the supernatural never appealed to me. As far as I'm concerned, it's like doing a crossword puzzle with a dictionary and thesaurus in front of you. It's cheating. If it's even possible.

But face it, I was at the end of my rope. The court declaring him dead was the last straw. I was so angry I was willing to try anything.

First, it was prayer. This from someone who hadn't been inside a church and meant it for maybe thirty years. This from a man who asks nothing from anyone. Begging favors isn't my style. But okay, extraordinary measures for extraordinary times. You watch enough of these million-dollar lottery winners thanking God for pulling their winning number and you think, well, maybe they're onto something. You think, hell, what could it hurt? So you get down on your knees and your fold your hands in supplication because that's the way these things are supposed to be done, and you click on religion and you humbly ask for something. You ask, in my case, for John Hartman.

And what are you willing to give in return (because there's

always a quid pro quo)? What do I have to give? What does God want these days? He wants everything. Okay? He wants you. He wants your soul. In my case, I don't figure I've got much use for mine anyway, so that's what I offered. For John Hartman, I offer my soul. I will be a good Christian. I will dedicate myself to Him. I will go to church every Sunday. God, do you know how tough that is for me to say? Do you know how tough it will be for me to do? But I'll do it. A deal's a deal. Charles Floyd will be reborn. Charles Floyd will join the legion of saps who live with Christ perched on their shoulders. Charles Floyd will do something he's never done before. Charles Floyd will believe in something other than himself. Charles Floyd will join the flock. He will admit that there is a higher power who can deliver the undeliverable, who can solve the unsolvable. He will BELIEVE! And you couldn't ask for anything more, could you?

I humbled myself in the face of God. And then I repeated the same routine for the next three days. Nothing. Okay, no one promised quick results. These things take time. But I am an impatient man. I decided to try another route. Another spiritual form. After all, how many times was I told as a kid that God helps those who help themselves? And how many times was I taught to cover all bases?

Her name was Katherine Seabury. She was well known amongst police departments up and down the East Coast. She had, according to those I questioned, some hits, some misses. For a psychic, though, her track record was pretty impressive. "She's uncanny," one Boston investigator told me. "She's not always 100 percent on the nose, but more often than not she'll tell you things either you didn't know that'll help you, or things she couldn't possibly know about the case. She made a believer out of me."

I had to be impressed. She took no money. Civic duty was all that propelled her. It was worth a try. I made an appointment.

She lived and worked out of a seedy, two-family wood-frame house in a rundown section of Newark, New Jersey. She wasn't what I expected. Instead of a mysterious-looking woman wrapped in veils and wearing a long, flowing gown, she was your typical Irish Catholic, working-class New Jersey housewife, about forty-five, slightly overweight, with mousey brown hair tied back in a bun. She was wearing a flower-print house dress with an apron over it. The house smelled of broiled chicken. She was making dinner, she told me. Psychics have to eat, too, she joked.

We sat at the kitchen table so she could keep an eye on the meal while it cooked. She was waiting for her two teenage kids to return from school. All the lights were on. We didn't hold hands. The table did not rise. I did not hear any disembodied voices of the dearly departed. No rattling chains. There were no mysterious raps or taps. No thumps or bumps. No crystal balls. The weather outside was perfect: bright and clear.

I asked her if she minded if I taped her and she said no.

I told her only that I was looking for a man. I did not tell her what he did, nor his name. She asked if I had anything that belonged to him. I gave her the original photograph of Hartman, which, for the past three years, I'd kept either in my wallet or in the night-table drawer beside my bed.

She took it without looking at it. She held it sandwiched between the palms of her hands. She closed her eyes and rubbed the photo between her hands gently. The room suddenly seemed remarkably still. And me with it. I realized I was holding my breath. I don't know why. I suppose maybe I was afraid of disturbing the spirits, or something like that.

Finally, after a couple minutes, she licked her lips, opened her eyes and said, "I'm confused."

"Why's that?"

"Because I'm getting mixed messages."

"What kinds of messages?"

"Would you like an apple?"

"Is that part of the process?"

"No. I just thought you might be hungry."

"I'm not. Let's continue. What kinds of messages?"

"You don't mind if I do, do you?"

"Do what?"

"Have an apple."

"No."

She put down the photograph and got up and got herself an apple. She sat down and took a bite.

"Well?" I said, anxious to get on with it.

"I think . . . it's very difficult . . . I think . . ." She took another bite. "I'm getting . . . traits . . . but they don't seem to mesh . . . I think maybe I'm dealing with two separate entities. Yes, two men. One is far from here. Very far. He is sitting in the dark. He's bent over. He's got pain . . . here," she said, pointing to her gut. "This man has killed. He's killed many times. One, two, three, four, five times. Five times, he's killed. With a gun. It happened years ago. In cold weather. There's another man, though . . . another man in pain. But it's a different kind of pain. This man is not far away. I sense him very strongly. He is very disturbed. Like the first man. They are the same, but they're different. Different men."

"Looks like you've got some interference in your reception," I said. "You're receiving two sets of vibes."

She put down the apple, picked up the photograph, closed her eyes and began gently caressing it again. "One of these men is you, Mr. Floyd."

"Me?"

"Yes. I'm getting your vibrations from this photograph. And they're stronger than the other man, who was the killer."

"I've owned the photo for over three years now, maybe that's why. But I don't want to know about me, Mrs. Seabury. I want to know about him, the other man, the man whose picture you've got there. The killer. I want to know where he is. Where is this dark room he's sitting in?"

She sighed, put down the photo and picked up her apple. "I don't think I can help you. I'm getting too many competing sensations. It's too hard for me to separate one from the other. It's a mishmash. I'm sorry. Maybe if you could find something that was his alone, maybe then I could help you."

"I don't have anything that was his alone. The weapons he used, maybe, but I don't have them with me. There's nothing else you can do for me?"

"Perhaps . . ."

"Well . . ."

"You have to understand, Mr. Floyd, I think that to some extent we all have this power. It's not a gift only given to a chosen few. Some of us have been able to hone the power more finely, that's all. It's a sense that can be trained. You have a very strong connection to this man."

"In a way."

"It's obvious. And perhaps we can use this connection, this connectivity, to help you find him."

"How's that?"

"I can teach you, Mr. Floyd. I can teach you how to use what you have. I can teach you to be a sensitive."

"Oh yeah? How long will it take?"

She laughed. "It's not like going to college. It's not four years, if that's what you're worried about. You don't get a degree. I can teach you in a matter of minutes. But it's like anything else. You must practice. You just can't learn to read music and then expect to become a concert pianist. You must have talent. You must practice. You must work at it."

"A few minutes, huh? Well, I can spare that. Teach me, Mrs.

Seabury. I'm yours."

She tried. First, she told me I had to make my mind a complete blank. She called it centering myself. I had to think of a blank wall, a blank piece of paper, a color. Okay. Next. I had to picture the man I was looking for against this blank wall or paper. Then I had to let my mind float free and picture him in any situation that popped into my head and then, like magic, little details about him would emerge. I'd see how he was dressed, maybe. Or I'd see the room he was in. Or who he was with. It was what she called an out-of-body experience. It sounded simple.

"It's not," she said.

"Then how do I know I'll be able to do it?"

"You don't. There are no guarantees. It's a technique, Mr. Floyd. Like anything else. And maybe if you get good enough at it you'll be able to find your man. I don't promise anything. I know you've checked me out enough to know that."

"Yes, I have, as a matter of fact. Listen, I'm not so sure about this. I feel funny . . ."

"Embarrassed?"

"Yeah, I guess. You read minds, huh?"

She laughed. "No. I have teenage kids, remember. I don't have the foggiest idea what they're thinking. If they're thinking. And if you're embarrassed, you don't have to tell anyone what you're doing."

"Believe me, I won't."

"It can work."

"Yeah, well, who knows." I got up to leave. "I hope you don't mind if maybe I call on you again. And if you get a call from him, I'm sure you'll let me know."

"It would be my pleasure," she said, smiling. "Would you like some fruit before you leave? Maybe for the drive back?"

"No, thanks."

"I hope you find what you're looking for, Mr. Floyd. I know it's very important to you."

"If he's alive, I'll find him . . . eventually."

"He's alive. You can be sure of that." She took a bite of her apple. "And he's waiting for you."

I wanted to ask her what she meant by that, but for some reason I didn't want to know. Maybe it was because it would have meant that I was totally buying into what she did, what she was. There was part of me, a big part, actually, that wanted to believe she could do what I hadn't been able to do for five years. But there was another part of me that scoffed at this whole supernatural thing. And that was the part that didn't ask her what she meant.

When I got home that evening, I decided to give it a whirl. It seemed ridiculous, but why not? At first, I had a devil of a time trying to wipe my mind clean. It's not easy. The slightest thing threw me off. The ticking of a clock. The sound of the wind outside my window. The creaking floors. An itch. A bird. Even the silence. Finally, after fifteen minutes, I gave up. Praying was infinitely easier. At least you could talk . . . and think. And deceive yourself into believing that someone, some thing, was actually listening.

Over the next week or two, whenever I had a few free minutes, I'd try again. Soon, I was able to do it. I couldn't hold it for long; but I could do it. The next step was to imagine Hartman, which wasn't nearly as difficult. That, I'd done at the house weeks before. By the third or fourth try, I had it. I'd get him a second . . . and then he was gone. But I got him. This sense of accomplishment made me feel better. It made me feel like I was doing something, not just spinning my wheels. I felt good afterward, like I'd gotten a full night's sleep, which I hadn't had in years. After a while, I'd "contact" him three, four, five times a day. It was as if he were part of me. I'd eat my dinner and imagine him eating his dinner, too. At any particular time of the day, no matter what I was doing, I'd try to imagine what he'd be doing. I could actually "feel" myself getting closer and closer to him, without ever leaving the state of Connecticut.

One day, I decided to add a new wrinkle, one of my own invention: a campaign of auto-suggestion. I figured once I conjured him up, once he was part of my consciousness, my life, why not just talk him back to Connecticut? So that's what I did. I kept putting the suggestion in his mind that he return. Over and over again, every time I "contacted" him, I'd urge him to come back. I'd imagine him getting on a plane or a train, or a bus, headed back to Sedgewick.

All this seemed to be doing a lot more than going the religious route, but, just the same, I hedged my bets by keeping up the prayer thing, too.

CHAPTER FORTY-EIGHT:
KATHERINE SEABURY

I didn't mind that he taped me. And I told him that I didn't think the spirits would mind, either. That was a joke. Believe me, when he took that thing home and played back the tape the only voices he was going to hear on it were his and mine. No spirits from the deep. No strange, unexplainable noises. No unexplained silences. I had a local television station here once. They were doing a report on the supernatural for Halloween. Since I was the closest thing they had to a ghost in the area, they decided they'd interview me. I'm afraid they were very disappointed. I wasn't about to be their performing dog. I don't read minds and I can't see into the future. Do you think, if I could, we'd still be living here? It's just that sometimes I can see and hear things other people don't. Or don't want to see or hear. I think I'm a lot closer to a forensic psychiatrist than I am to one of those so-called mentalists, like Kreskin. But I get a real kick out of him. All those mind-reading tricks he does, especially the one where you hide his check and then either he finds it or doesn't get paid. That wouldn't work with me, though, because I don't take any money.

That Mr. Floyd came and asked for my help—he didn't really want to come, but I could see he was at the end of his rope and he didn't know what else to do. That's usually when law enforcement comes to me; after they've tried everything else. When the pressure is on them to solve a case and they don't have any other leads. When they've exhausted all the conventional ways of solving the crime. But I don't promise to help them. Sometimes I have, but sometimes I just can't see what they want me to see. And I want to make this clear again. I don't take money or anything else for what I do, when I do it. I do it because they ask me and because I don't have a choice, really. If you were out riding in your car and you saw an accident, wouldn't you call for help? That's what I do. When someone's in trouble and they need my help and I can help them, I do.

It's not something I work at. It just happens. It's kind of like a heightened form of intuition. Or sometimes, I compare it to time travel. When the vibrations—because that's what I call it, though that's not really what it is—when the vibrations are right, then I find myself, or my psyche, really, floating through the air, to where the crime happened, or to where the missing person is. And then, I'm hovering over it, like a helicopter or something, and I can slowly lower myself down, till I'm right there, in the middle of things. I can then see the thing happen, or I can see the person I'm looking for.

It's complicated and it's simple and I wish I could explain it better, but I can't. And I truly believe, as I told Mr. Floyd, that to some extent all of us have this "power," but like any other talent, some have it more than others, and some can hone it by working harder at it. I tried to teach him, but I don't know if he got it.

The truth is, I could sense that Mr. Floyd is a very confused and troubled man. I could feel that when he was here. And one of the reasons I couldn't get a read on that Hartman man was because the vibes I was getting from Mr. Floyd were so strong.

What do I think is going to happen with John Hartman? Well, that's a good question. First of all, I'm pretty sure he's alive. It's not something I know. It's something I feel. And although I can't tell you why, I have this sneaking suspicion that at some point, and I don't know when and I don't know why, he's going to be back in the news again.

And as for where he is, well, I have this sense that he's in a warm place. A place where they don't speak English. I'm getting Latin vibes. That's what I'm getting.

I wish I could tell you more, but I just can't.

CHAPTER FORTY-NINE:
CHARLIE FLOYD

James Kirkland, the fellow who lived across the street from the Hartmans, and his wife were vacationing in Buenos Aires for the Christmas holiday. While they were doing some late-afternoon shopping, Mr. Kirkland swore he saw Hartman walking down the street. It had been just a shade over three years since the murders and, though we'd occasionally get word of a Hartman sighting, most of them in Europe now, not one ever turned out to be anything other than a false alarm. But this, I thought, was different. This was a sighting by someone who actually knew him.

I was excited. It was the first real break in the case in nearly two years. No one cares anymore. No one, that is, except me. I care. Boy, do I care. It's like I was still carrying the torch for an old lover. Though I've handled dozens and dozens of cases since that one, I still care enough to carry John Hartman's creased and crumbling snapshot around with me in my wallet. And I cared enough to be at the Kirklands' home the day after they returned from Argentina, only several hours after they reported what Mr. Kirkland said he'd seen.

The circumstances were these: His wife was in some leather goods store looking at purses while Mr. Kirkland waited outside. He was girl-watching when suddenly his attention was diverted across the street where he thought he saw someone who looked familiar. "There was just something about him," said Mr. Kirk-land. "Something that made me know right away that it was him. Maybe it was the way he walked, the way he held his body. I don't think I could have been mistaken." At that point, Kirkland shouted into the store to his wife what he'd seen and then he took off after the man he thought was Hartman. He called out his name, but he was probably too far away and so there was no response. Eventually, without ever getting close enough to see his face, Kirkland lost him in the crowd.

"Are you sure it was him?" I asked.

"As sure as I could be under the circumstances."

His wife was there, too, sitting on the couch beside him. I asked her, "Did you see him?"

"No. I was inside."

I turned back to Kirkland. "You couldn't have been mistaken, could you?"

"I suppose I could have, but I don't think I was."

I drove away convinced Hartman was in Argentina and, if he hadn't been aware he'd been spotted by Kirkland, which seemed likely, he might still be there. I went back to my office and asked Ed if I could go to Argentina to bring him back.

"Absolutely not," he said without blinking an eye.

"Why not?"

"You have to ask?"

"Yes."

"Because this is a three-year-old case and I'm not about to send you all the way the hell down to Argentina on something as flimsy as an ID by a man who was no closer than a hundred feet on a crowded street. Think about it. Doesn't it sound a little incredible to you?"

"Your answer is final?"

"You bet. About as final as it can get."

"All right then, I've got some time coming to me, don't I?"

"It wouldn't surprise me."

"Well, I want to take it now."

"Charles, you're crazy. You're going to go down there at your own expense on something as flaky as this? You're crazy."

"It's my business, Ed. My time, my money, my business. It's something I've got to do."

"Your bête noire, I think they call it."

"That's right."

"Well, I'm not even going to go to the trouble of trying to talk you out of it. You want to go, then go. It's summer down there, the women are hot, so I guess it won't be a total loss. At least you'll come back with a tan."

So I went. Spent six days down there and must have walked a hundred miles. I showed his photo around, inquiring if anyone had seen anyone who looked even remotely like it. Nothing. I hung out, day and night, on the streets, in cafés, in bars, hoping to bump into him. I questioned all the Americans and English-speaking people I could find, hoping he might have gravitated toward them. I even tried what worked for me in Mexico City, the bookstores. Nothing.

I began to lose heart. I didn't want to return to Connecticut a failure. What was to be my last day in Argentina I spent alone in my hotel room, sitting in the dark, despondent, frustrated, powerless, ashamed. I even considered chucking it all, quitting my job, never returning to Connecticut. Fuck it.

A few hours before my flight home I shook myself from this mood, at least temporarily, and gave it one more try out on the streets. It was noon time and the sidewalks were jammed with people. I tried to look at every one of them. My eyes ached. My head throbbed. Bottom line: no Hartman.

I got on that plane still convinced that he was alive. That I might even have passed him in the street. Or maybe he'd buried himself so deep and so well that the likes of me would never find him. Oh, I suppose it could've been Hartman that Kirk-land had seen, but if it was he might have been just passing through, and I didn't have the time or resources to fan out through the countryside looking for him.

He might have melted into another dimension, for all I knew.

I felt like a fool when I returned home. It was tough to face the boys back at the office. Ed was very cool about it. He just asked me if I'd recommend Argentina for a holiday.

Chapter Fifty:
James Kirkland

Yesterday, my wife comes to me while I'm thinking about taking out the screens and putting up the storm windows, before we get that big blast of winter, and says, "Jim, I want to talk to you about something."

"Okay," I say, "talk." I said this because I was happy for any interruption of a ritual I truly despise.

"Now, I want you to think about this before you give me an answer."

"Don't I always?"

"Let's not be funny."

"Okay, we'll be serious then. See, I've got my serious face on. Now, what is it you want to talk about?"

"The house."

"Okay, the house. That's a pretty serious subject. What is it you want to say about the house? It's not on fire, is it?"

"You promised . . ."

"Right. Serious. Now, seriously, what is it about the house?"

"It's too big."

"Yes, I suppose some might consider it a bit ostentatious, but I call it home. Besides, it's very difficult to shrink a house."

"I'm serious, Jim."

"So am I. I do call it home."

"Okay, I'll continue."

"Please do."

"The kids are out of the house now and I don't think we

need such a big place for just the two of us. It's impossible to heat, it's impossible to clean, and it's completely unnecessary. I was talking to Jill Nelson the other day. Did you know she went into real estate?"

"I do now, though I can't imagine her actually working at anything."

"Well, anyway, I was talking to her and she thinks we could easily get $2 million plus for the house. But it's not just the money. It's the practicality of the whole thing. I mean, what do we need with a place like this? It just doesn't make sense. It's a case of conspicuous consumption, pure and simple."

"Have you been taking an economics course behind my back? You're not afraid of what the neighbors might think, are you? You're not afraid that they'll think we're in here all day consuming conspicuously, are you? Because both of us know nothing could be further from the truth."

"What happened to serious, Jim?"

"Okay, seriously. I've lived in this house for what, twenty-two years now? It's my home and I don't think I want to give it up. Millions or not. Besides, where would we go from here?"

"Where? My God, Jim, use your imagination. There are plenty of places. We could move to Hartford, down to Greenwich, Westport, or even New York City."

"You hate New York City."

"I don't hate New York. I just didn't think it was the right place to bring up a family. Listen, we'll have plenty of money. We could even buy a small place by the Sound and use it as a summer place."

"Now that's what I call conspicuous consumption."

"You know what I mean."

"You know this house means a lot to me. Some of the best times of my life were spent here . . . except for putting up storm windows. I don't know whether I could leave it so easily. My life history's part of this house, and the house is a part of me. You know, in some kind of weird way I sometimes think this house defines me as a person. I mean, look what we went through together in this house."

"You mean, like the Hartman thing?"

I stopped for a moment. "Yes, I suppose the Hartman thing enters into it."

"That's sick, Jim. You know that? I mean, to think that the most exciting thing in your life is a murder that took place across the street years ago, well that's just the sickest thing I think I've ever heard. And you know, I think it's one of the reasons I want to sell this place and move on. I've never felt comfortable here since the night they found the bodies. It's not that I'm afraid of his coming back. It's more that I saw something in you I didn't like. It changed you . . . and not for the better. You know, sometimes I think that that single night made your life worth living . . ."

"That's ridiculous," I said, but I'm not sure I said it with all the conviction I'd meant to.

CHAPTER FIFTY-ONE:
JOHN HARTMAN

One day, for no reason I could put my finger on, I just packed up a suitcase, threw it in the back of my car, pulled out of the driveway and began to drive. At first, I wasn't quite sure where I was going.

But it would soon become apparent.

Chapter Fifty-Two:
Sheriff Tillman

It was a screw-up, all right, but you couldn't exactly say it was all our fault. Blame it on the system, if you like. This fella gets brought in here on a simple drunk and disorderly and the next thing we know he's confessing to damn near every murder that ever took place in the entire state of Texas in the last five years. Now when someone does that and knows as much about them murders as he did, then we got to take him seriously. Because what we got here is either a real student of homicide, someone who's read up on just about every local murder case of any significance, or someone who's done himself a whole mess of killing.

Now I don't want anyone to think we're some kind of hick operation down here, because we ain't. We know what we're doing. We know that just because someone confesses to something don't mean he actually went and done it. We're well into the twenty-first century, sure enough. We know all about compulsions and obsession and all that high-falutin' psychological mumbo-jumbo. Hey, where you think Dr. Phil gets that funny accent from? But just the same, we got to check everything out, so that's just what we did. And it didn't take long before we decided that although many of his so-called confessions had the ring of truth to them, he was not our guy. He just didn't know enough about any one individual case. Nothing that hadn't been in the papers. Nothing he couldn't have gone to the library or online and read about. And every time we tried to get him to get specific, he just couldn't quite recall the details. His memory took a very convenient holiday, you might say. But listen, after all was said and done, I didn't have much doubt that somewhere along the line this guy might well have actually killed someone. It just wasn't our someone. I don't know what it was about him, but he reeked of it. I been at this long enough to know a killer when I see him. But killed who and when, that was the question. Listen, I'm no genius. It stood to reason, when you gave it some thought. Why else would someone go to all the trouble of boning up on murder?

But in this country you can't hold someone indefinitely just 'cause you got a gut feeling. We got laws against that. This is still America, you understand. Though sometimes you wouldn't know it, from what goes on. And so, after he spent a couple of days in the clink, we got to let him loose. It's as simple as that. The best I can do is escort him to the edge of town, suggest to him that he never show us the front side of himself again, give 'im a little push in the right direction—the hell outta here—and then he's someone else's problem. So, essentially, that's just what I done.

He said his name was Lawrence Sedgewick Borden and he had the papers to back him up—Social Security card, driver's license, even a Sears credit card. A course, they coulda been phonies . . . and, as it turns out, they was. According to his driver's license, Borden was 52, but he appeared to be closer to 60, which added to my doubts about his confession, and it occurred to me that his documents could've been phony. He was of average height, thin, gaunt-looking, with longish, unkempt gray hair and a scraggly salt-and-pepper beard. Not unlike the kind of drifters we see comin' on through here all the time. Looked like he was suffering from malnutrition and hadn't seen a bar of soap in a dog's age. He was well spoken, though, obviously educated, but he had a tendency to ramble. Then, suddenly, he'd stop talking, stare out into space, and totally clam up. But he was cooperative. Too cooperative.

We took prints and sent 'em off to the proper authorities, but here's where the screw-up took place. They didn't come back in time. His legal aid lawyer saw to it that he was let go and our part of the screw-up was that we saw through his lies too quick. If we'd been a little slower, we coulda held him on suspicion, but since we knew he didn't commit none of them, where was the suspicion?

He had twenty-seven bucks in his wallet. I don't know why, but I kinda felt sorry for him. I know I already said I thought he was probably guilty of killin' somebody, but there was just something about him. Besides, I said I thought he was a killer, which don't mean he actually was one. Lotsa people look like they killed someone or could kill someone, you know. Anyways, I took him to the bus station in my black and white. On the way, we had what technically qualifies as a short, off-the-record conversation.

"You ought to be ashamed of yourself," I said.

"I am," he said, his head bowed, his voice so low I could hardly hear him.

"You know, you caused us a hell of a lot of trouble—and taxpayers' money. You may not think so, but we got better things to do than go on wild goose chases. What's with you, anyway?"

"I'm guilty and I just want my punishment to end."

"End? Buddy, I got news for you, if we thought you was guilty of any of them things you confessed to, our punishment woulda just begun. In this here state we got us the death penalty and we ain't afraid to use it."

"I am guilty . . ."

"Of what?"

"Crimes against humanity. Crimes against nature. Crimes against God."

"Well, that just about covers everything, I guess," I said. "Maybe you want to be a little more specific?"

"I can't be more specific. You understand what humanity is, don't you?"

"I think I used to before I took this job, but now I'm not so sure."

He was staring out the window. Now I got to admit something I'm not particularly proud of. I got to admit I coulda pulled that ole black and white over to the side of the road and sat there and talked with Mr. Borden or whatever his name was for what, maybe ten, fifteen minutes more, and maybe I woulda got something. But I didn't want to do it. I considered it, I really did, but something told me ten or fifteen minutes more with this fella woulda complicated my life more than I ever woulda wanted it to be complicated. Sure, I was curious, but not that curious. Besides, it was late in the day and I was hungry and my wife was expectin' me home. Still, I couldn't help askin' him where he was headed.

"East."

"Whereabouts?"

"New England."

"Nice area. Been up there once. Got family there maybe?"

"Not anymore. But there are people waiting for me."

"Well, that's nice. But how you gonna get there on twenty-seven dollars is beyond me."

"I don't know."

I thought a minute. I had a feeling it was important to get where he was going. This was not policy, but I said, "How about I lend you a few bucks? You can send it back to me when you get where you're going."

"No," he said.

We was in front of the bus depot now. I took out my wallet and counted up what I had. More than I thought. I unlocked the door and he got out. I followed him. He was just standing on the sidewalk. I took his arm and led him into the bus station. We walked up to the ticket seller. "Where is it you want to go?" I asked.

"As far as what I have will take me," he said.

"But where exactly is it you want to end up?"

"In hell, where I belong."

"Well, unfortunately none of these here buses are headed in that direction, so give me another destination."

He thought for a moment. "Connecticut," he said. "New Haven. Connecticut."

I repeated this to the ticket seller and asked how much. She told me. I counted out the money and got him his ticket. At first, he wouldn't take it. I insisted. "Don't worry, I'll get it back, one way or another. Even if it's from petty cash."

So he took the ticket and I put him on the bus myself, just to make sure he didn't cash it in and spend it on booze or something. He didn't actually thank me with words, but I could see that he appreciated what I done.

It wasn't until three days later that we got the report from the federal authorities. Our Mr. Borden was really John Hartman, a fugitive wanted for murder, a man who'd been presumed dead for almost two years.

Hell, after seeing him, after spending time with him like I did, as far as I was concerned he might as well have been.

Chapter Fifty-Three:
Charlie Floyd

Janie McClellan was in town. She called the office and left a message for me. Three years have passed. Like the snap of a finger. Three years. Count the creases on my face and you'd think it was more, though.

The message was sitting there on my desk. A pink slip. Under the notation, While You Were Out, was her name and a number where she could be reached. I stared at it for several moments, thinking of her, picturing her, wondering what she looked like now.

But Janie came in a package, a package that included John Hartman. She was a constant reminder that I'd failed in my attempts to find him. It was my fault. There must have been things I could have done, I should have done, that I didn't. It was my fault he was getting away with it.

I didn't call her right back. I didn't want to have to face her just then. I was ashamed, I suppose. It didn't make sense. But I was.

The day after she called I was sitting in my car in the parking lot. My hands were on the wheel and I was just staring ahead, wondering where I was going. Suddenly, I had this strange feeling in the pit of my stomach. There was a tightness that was spreading through the rest of my body. Something seemed to be growing inside me, expanding, larger and larger. I began to shake. There was something in there, under my skin, trying to consume me, trying to get out. I thought I was having a heart attack. I tried to fight it. I clenched my fists, my teeth. I tried to fight back the invader. This thing that was trying to devour me.

I was losing the battle.

The thing, whatever it was, was expanding outward and upward, to my mind. It was taking me over. I began to have incredibly violent thoughts. I thought of Janie McClellan. I pictured her with me. She was standing in front of me, taunting me. "You're nothing," she was saying. "You can't even find John. You can't bring him back. You can't protect me. You can't protect anyone. What good are you?" The look on her face was one of disdain. I shrunk from it. I felt myself getting smaller and smaller. I wanted to run. I wanted to hide. She turned her back on me.

I put my head in my hands and pressed hard on my temples, trying to squeeze out the demon that was in there. Harder and harder, I pressed. And then I stopped. And I thought it was gone.

But it wasn't gone. It was still there and when I thought of Janie McClellan I thought of killing her. I wanted her to stop contacting me. I wanted her to be out of my life. Forever. I . . . or the thing inside me, the thing that was under my skin, began to imagine how I would do it, how I could do it without being caught. I would get a gun that couldn't be traced. I would meet her out in the woods somewhere. I would shoot her once. In the head. I would shoot her so that I couldn't see the look on her face anymore. I would squeeze the trigger. I would shoot her. I would see her falling over. As if in slow motion, I would see blood splatter on my shirt, my jacket. I would see the new look of surprise on her face as she fell. I would pull the trigger again . . . and again . . . and again. I would shoot at her face until it was just a bloody mess, until I would see the inside of her skull, until there would be nothing left but bloody tissue. Until there would be no look on her face at all . . . But it wasn't really her.

I knew that. It was John Hartman I wanted gone.

I was frightened. My hands were damp with perspiration. My heart was beating loudly in my chest. Thump. Thump. Thump. It went. My shirt was drenched. I hit the car horn and held it down for several seconds, trying to put a stop to whatever was happening. As if the sound of a horn would chase away the demons. People walking through the lot stared at me, angry looks on their faces. I stopped. I waited for the thing inside me to start up again. But it was gone. I was alone. Under my skin, I was alone. Finally. Alone.

She called again and left another message. But I ignored it.

That was two weeks ago. Maybe she's still in town. Maybe she's back for good. Maybe the number, which I carry around in my wallet, right next to John Hartman's photograph, is still good. Maybe I'll get around to dialing it. Maybe.

But not now. Not yet.

*

CHAPTER FIFTY-FOUR:
CHARLIE FLOYD

Last night, I was lying in the dark on the couch with my eyes closed. I was waiting for something. I don't know what. Suddenly, an image came to me on the inside of my eyelids, as clear as a bell. I was on Main Street in Sedgewick. There was a man standing across the street, his back to me, peering into a shop window. A grocery store. I could see boxes of Oxydol detergent stacked one on top of the other, forming a pyramid. I crossed the street and came up behind him. He was wearing a dark blue suit. The suit fit poorly. It was much too big for him. There was some lint on his shoulder. His shoes needed a shine. When I got closer, I saw that his hair came well below his collar. I put my hand on his shoulder and squeezed. It was soft and mushy, like a wet sponge. He seemed to shrink under my touch and suddenly I was left holding mostly fabric. He made a half turn and I finally saw his face. He had a goofy, child-like grin. He put his arms out to the side, like they were airplane wings. He dropped his head to one side so that it rested on his shoulder.

"Gotcha," I said, pointing my finger at him like it was a gun. He smiled.

Chapter Fifty-Five:
Sergeant Diggett

I was on weekend shift. It was Saturday morning. You'd think weekends would be easy, kinda slow, laid-back, you know, the kinda day when you could just sit there readin' the paper, sucking up the caffeine. But not. That's not the way it is. In fact, weekends are just about our busiest time. Crime never takes a holiday. But if it did, it certainly wouldn't be on a weekend.

It was about ten o'clock in the morning, I suppose. And it was busy as hell. Friday night'd been a hot one, unseasonably hot, and between the kids drinkin' beer and gettin' into all kinds of mischief, and the adults, at least that's what they pretend to be, lettin' off steam, we were really jumpin'.

So that's why I didn't see him come in. I really can't say the first time I noticed him. Maybe it was when one of the other officers came in and called out a hello.

But then I did see him. He was standing near the door, leaning up against the wall. He was looking in my direction, but he wasn't really looking at me. Do you understand what I mean? I mean, his head was pointed at me, but his eyes seemed to be someplace in the back of his skull. I thought maybe he was lost. Needed directions somewhere. But it was much too busy for me to find out. If he had a problem, let him come to me. That's what I thought.

The next time I noticed him, he was standing in the middle of the room. Same expression. Or non-expression. A weirdo, that's what I figured he was. Or maybe he was on something. I made a mental note to myself to keep an eye on him. Just in case. We once had a guy come in here and wave around a gun. Two officers pounced on him before he could do any damage. Turned out it was just one of those starter guns, but how were we to know that?

Anyway, a few minutes pass and I look up and now he's standing right in front of me.

"Can I help you?" I say.

"I can help you," he says.

"Is that so?"

He nods.

"How's that?"

"You're looking for me."

"That so?"

He nods.

"And what am I looking for you for?"

"Are you in charge?" he asks.

I smile and look around. "As far as you're concerned I am. Now why am I looking for you?"

He takes a piece of paper out of his pocket, unfolds it and puts it on my desk, smoothing it out with his hands. I look at it. It's an old, yellowed newspaper clipping. It's got a picture of a guy on it. It's about this murder case that happened three years ago, before I was even on the job. It's about a guy named Hartman.

I shrug. "You got information about this guy?" I ask.

He gets this agitated look on his face. "Don't you see?" he says.

"Relax, pal. I see fine. Now what is it you want? Can't you see I'm pretty busy here?"

"You want . . ."

"All right, what is it I want?"

"Me."

Now, I'm starting to lose patience.

"It's me," he says, pointing to the photograph. "Can't you see?"

I look down. I look up. To tell the truth, I can't see any resemblance. None at all. This guy in front of me looks like death warmed over. He hasn't shaved in a week, maybe more, and his cheeks are sunken and he's somewhere inside that blue suit he's wearing, but I'm not sure where.

"Are you telling me that you're this guy, John Hartman? Is that what you're telling me?"

He nods. I look at the photo again. I look at the eyes. I concentrate on them. Then I look at the eyes of the guy in front of me. Then it hits me. He's right. He is the guy. And he's standing right in front of me. John Hartman. The guy who murdered his family. He's right there in front of me and he's giving himself up.

I want to get up from my chair, but I can't. I want to draw my gun, but I can't. I just sit there with my mouth hanging open.

For the first time the guy in front of me, John Hartman, gets an expression on his face. He starts to smile. I've got John Hartman in front of me and he's smiling.

"Hey," I shout to no one in particular. "We got him. We got John Hartman!"

Chapter Fifty-Six:
John Hartman

Finally.

I am home.

It's over.

Finally.

ABOUT THE AUTHOR

Charles Salzberg is a freelance writer whose work has appeared in *New York* magazine, *GQ, Esquire, The New York Times, Elle, Ladies Home Journal, Redbook* and other periodicals. He has been a Visiting Professor of Magazine at the S.I. School of Public Communications at Syracuse University, has taught writing at Sarah Lawrence College and Hunter College, and he now teaches at the Writer's Voice and the New York Writers Workshop, where he is a founding member. His novel *Swann's Last Song* was nominated for a Shamus Award for Best First PI Novel. The sequel, *Swann Dives In,* was published in 2012 as a Five Star Mystery.